Sparrow Days

Sparrow Days

Russell Sebring

CURIOUS CURLS PUBLISHING

Curious Curls Publishing
CuriousCurlsPublishing.com
@CuriousCurlsPub

Sebring, Russell.
Sparrow Days / Russell Sebring
ISBN 978-1-958373-06-4 (paperback)
Print: July 2023

Cover Illustration by Nikita Kaun

*For all the brilliant young minds in the world,
who suffer the repression of growing up where
there is seemingly little to inspire the soul,
and no guidance or encouragement.
Don't despair or let others steal your dreams.
There is radiance everywhere,
and a passing breeze.
Feather your own wings, and fly.
Make your own luck,
and know that I believe in you.*

1

"Where's the girl?" asked Officer Carroll. Out of habit, he took off his glasses, extracted an old tissue from his pants pocket, and cleaned them.

It was a little past midnight. In his thirty-plus years on the police force, the married officer and father of three couldn't recall an evening this quiet. There had been no break-ins, domestic disputes, or major trouble of any kind. Other than pulling over two drivers for speeding and helping reroute traffic at the scene of a minor car accident, all had been relatively calm—that is, until a few minutes ago, when a dispatch had come in, requesting he investigate a situation at the Fast Mart. The manager had called to report a young girl, alone and apparently determined to spend the night, inside the store. She might be a runaway.

Glancing around the brightly-lit twenty-four-hour convenience store, Officer Carroll yawned. There was a chain reaction. First, Felipe, the overnight manager, stretched out his arms and let loose a rather noisy yawn of his own. Then all three customers standing in line at the register, ready to pay for their items, yawned in turn.

"She's back there." Felipe gestured toward the rear of the store, where the milk, soft drinks, and beer were kept in a long row of refrigerated coolers.

"Thanks." The officer stepped aside to let someone who had just bought three scratch-off lottery tickets and a bag of sour cream-and-onion potato chips past him. He put his glasses back on, touched his leather gun holster lightly—another habit—and made his way to the back of the store.

He quietly stepped around the corner of the last aisle. Sitting on the tile floor, cross-legged, her back resting against a shelf stocked with packaged pastries and bread, was a young girl. A large camouflage jacket was draped over her body, and her eyes were closed.

Officer Carroll smiled. The sleeping child looked so at peace; he didn't want to disturb her. Instead, he imagined bringing her a fluffy pillow and wrapping her in a blanket. But he had a job to do: he needed to find out who she was. If necessary, he was prepared to give her a ride home. According to radio dispatch, the girl had been lingering inside the store for several hours, and no one recognized her.

"Ahem!" Officer Carroll cleared his throat, hoping to gently rouse her, but the girl didn't move. Her content, tranquil expression remained the same.

He stood in front of her and lightly nudged her leg with his foot. "Ahem…" Three gentle prods more, each a little firmer, and gradually the girl stirred. Her nose twitched, and her eyes opened.

"Hello, miss," Officer Carroll said warmly. "May I ask what your name is?"

She stared into his eyes but didn't answer him.

"You can't stay here. You know that, right?" he added. "And there's a local curfew for kids." No response. "You're much too young to be out this late by yourself. Where do you live?" Nothing.

The girl looked up at him, unfazed. Officer Carroll decided to try a different approach. "How old are you? I'd say you look maybe six years old."

"I'm eight!" said the girl. She crossed her arms and frowned. Her cheeks turned pink.

Officer Carroll tried hard not to laugh. "Does anyone know you're here?" No answer. He took a moment to think. "I'm not going to hurt you. Maybe we can make a deal. If you tell me your name, I'll buy you something to eat or drink. How does that sound?"

Hesitantly, she answered, "Terra."

"Pretty name." Officer Carroll knew he was making some headway. "So, my lovely Miss Terra, can you tell me why you're sleeping on the floor in a Fast Mart and on a school night?"

It was now officially Tuesday morning, Valentine's Day. The officer rubbed his hands together, another habit. It was twenty-five degrees outside, the chill emanating from the coolers reminding him of how cold the night was.

They exchanged glances, neither saying a word for a time. Maybe it was just a few moments, but it felt much longer than that. The front doors of the Fast Mart could be heard opening and closing while friendly voices spoke near the cash register. The sounds would stop, and soon they could be overheard again.

"Are you hungry?" asked Officer Carroll. "The Star Diner is always open." Terra nodded and sluggishly rose to her feet. As she did, the officer saw a nametag sewn on the front of the heavy green camouflage jacket she held. It was a US Army field jacket; the tag above the pocket on the right side of the chest read, "Delarosa."

"Does that belong to your dad?" he asked as Terra struggled to put on the jacket. Clearly made for an adult, it was many sizes too big for her. The bottom of it reached below her knees.

"It did," she said. "But now it belongs to me. My mom gave it to me after he died."

"Oh, I'm very sorry." Officer Carroll didn't know quite what else to say. "I'm sure your father was a good man. How long ago did this happen?"

"He got killed by a bomb when I was a baby. I don't remember him. My mom says he was mean sometimes when he came home. All I know is what Mom tells me about my dad. He might have been nice, I guess."

She paused. Looking at her, Officer Carroll imagined he could actually see the memories and hurt cascading inside the girl's mind like a waterfall. But then again, maybe he was wrong. Terra added, "He was a soldier driving a truck. It happened in Afghanistan."

"And where's your mom? Why aren't you at home?"

"You've got her," answered Terra.

"What does that mean?" asked Officer Carroll. "I don't have your mom. Who is she?"

"One of you arrested her. They took my mom away and put her in jail. You got her. I get to see her just sometimes. Her name is Mary."

"Where do you live now? Who takes care of you?" Once again, there was no answer. Young Terra Delarosa had rebuilt her wall of silence.

Officer Carroll stepped away, held down a button on a two-way radio clipped near his badge, and talked to someone on the other end. He kept his voice low and spoke in bits and pieces. "Yeah…I understand…Roger that." Terra was listening. He turned his back to her.

"What are you doing?" asked Terra. She came closer to him. Officer Carroll sensed the girl was starting to panic, but didn't answer her. He continued his call, listening and methodically speaking. Then he felt something. There was a small, quick tug at his side, and he heard a click.

Officer Carroll looked down. His holster was empty. He spun around and came face-to-face with the barrel of his own gun. Shaking, Terra had both hands on the loaded Glock, pointing it at his head.

"I'm not going back!" she screamed. Her face was turning red, her body trembling.

"Whoa! Please don't!" Shocked and uncertain of what to say or do next, Officer Carroll stood frozen, staring into the eyes of the innocent-looking eight-year-old who now held his life in her hands.

2

At dawn, there was a tiny tap, tap, tap at the bedroom window. Cyrus Kane pulled the covers over his aching head, buried his ears into the layers of warmth, and desperately tried to ignore the sound. But like every morning for the past year, this insistent little noise wasn't going to stop. *Tap...tap.* He turned over and cursed the sunlight. His eyes opened.

He threw on pants and a shirt and opened the window. "Get in quick!" groaned Cyrus. "You're going to let in all the cold."

A bright-colored sparrow hopped through a small hole cut in the screen and onto the dusty windowsill. It fluffed its feathers, looked around, and flew to the dresser.

Cyrus flopped back down into bed. He felt ragged and beat up. Nearly every muscle of his aging body seemed to hurt. He resisted waking, but as usual, a few more minutes of shuteye wasn't possible. His pocket-sized friend was on his head, stepping lightly across his tousled gray hair to the edge of his scraggly face. His eyebrows were being plucked clean.

"Zeezoo! What did I tell you about this? Get off me!" He shooed the bird away and sat up. Zeezoo flew back to the dresser and waited. It was the same ritual nearly every morning. "Are you hungry?" asked Cyrus. "Of course you are. How about I make us some bacon and…eggs." Cyrus mussed his hair and got up. He laughed all the way to the kitchen. Zeezoo raced to beat him there.

It wasn't long before the sweet and salty smell of a hot breakfast attracted Edgar, the old striped tomcat. He scratched at the back door and whined. Cyrus let him in. A dish of milk and some pungent cat food were waiting. At the kitchen table, Zeezoo was eating leftover canned peas and a French fry. After every few bites, he hopped to the table's edge and looked down to see where Edgar was. He had learned to keep a wary eye on the always-mischievous feline.

"Edgar" was short for "Edgar Allan Poe." Over the years, he had used up at least six or seven of his nine lives, the first one at birth. One day, while Cyrus was scrounging for odds and ends behind a warehouse, he heard a faint crying and found the newborn kitten in a cardboard box that had been placed next to a county dumpster. There were six kittens in the box. Edgar was the lone survivor.

"Zeezoo, I've been thinking," said Cyrus. He took a sip straight from a nearly empty bottle of whiskey, set it back down, and stuffed an enormous piece of bacon into his mouth. "You need a girlfriend. It's time you found yourself a wife, someone you can build a nest together with, maybe raise a few babies."

Zeezoo understood, of course. But sparrow words aren't translatable into human language. And except for a few exceptional bird lovers who instinctively know but can't explain how they understand to anyone else, no one has solved the problem. Not yet, anyway. Zeezoo chirped twice. Cyrus Kane wasn't quite sure, but after hanging around the bird for a while now, he had begun to wonder if maybe one chirp meant "no" and two meant "yes." If so, it meant Zeezoo agreed with him.

Edgar was listening too. In truth, animals instinctively understand and can communicate with all other species. It's only humans who are confused.

After gulping his food, Edgar discreetly moved to a spot underneath the table. Unseen, he patiently lay in wait. Before long, a stray pea rolled off Zeezoo's plate onto the floor. Cyrus was standing next to the stove. It happened in an instant. Zeezoo spotted the dropped pea and went after it. Edgar pounced, claws out, teeth ready to chomp. Suddenly, the cat felt the painful sting of a metal spatula on his backside, hissed, and jumped away. In one quick motion, Cyrus grabbed Edgar by the scruff of his neck, carried him to the door, and tossed him out.

"How many times have I warned you, Edgar?" shouted Cyrus angrily. "How many times? I told you! This bird is off limits to you. Get away from here!"

With Edgar wailing and racing off in the direction of the barn, Cyrus spun around to see two or three feathers on the floor and Zeezoo standing on the table, his beak around the pea. "Are you all right?" he asked.

Zeezoo set aside the pea and chirped twice.

Except for Edgar, three chickens, two goats, and a crippled mare he had rescued from being put down, Cyrus lived alone. His nearest neighbors were more than two miles away. He had tacked up a KEEP OUT sign on a fencepost along the main highway, and not many people were brave enough to ignore it. As far as visitors were concerned, only Zeezoo came and went as he wished.

The once-thriving farm had been in the Kane family for four generations. At various times, there had been sheep and cattle grazing, dairy cows waiting to be milked, and a pen filled with pigs getting fatter as they wallowed in thick mud within a few yards of the smokehouse. There had been a rooster crowing atop the chicken coop, and in the distance, the fields had seen rotations of sweet corn, wheat, and soybeans.

All that was gone. Cyrus no longer cared about the land's potential. He couldn't think of a reason to begin again. He spent most days in solitude, slowly drinking his life away. Everything around him lay in disrepair. A rusted tractor, too ancient to fix, waited in the sun for the earth to eventually claim it. And not far from the main house, one could discern the silhouette of a vegetable garden overrun by weeds. But even though nothing had been planted for almost a decade, the occasional green bean, bell pepper, or tomato could still be found growing wild.

The sun was directly overhead, just beginning to warm what was left of the day from behind a colorless winter sky, when the drone of tires could be heard coming up the dirt road. A car pulled in next to the farmhouse, and a short middle-aged woman dressed in a light gray suit and holding a sizable briefcase stepped out. Watching from a window, Cyrus waited for her to knock and was slow to open the door. He let her wait for more than two minutes, hoping she'd turn around and leave.

He finally gave in and opened the door halfway. "Who are you?" asked Cyrus gruffly.

"Hello. Sorry to bother you. I'm Roberta Johnson," the woman answered. She spoke in an unhurried, methodic tone. "Are you Cyrus Kane?"

"That's me. What do you want?"

"First, I'm not sure if you're aware of it, Mr. Kane, but you're a difficult person to reach." Roberta stood outside the door like she had taken root there. She wasn't going away. "Please excuse the intrusion, but we need to talk, and I couldn't find another way to contact you. Don't you have a cell phone? Do you have email or a computer?"

"I don't believe in computers," he answered. "They're ruining the world. And that goes for cell phones too. I don't own a phone anymore. I hate the sight of them."

"You might be right, Mr. Kane," Roberta responded. "I believe innovation and technology can both enhance the quality of our lives and destroy things. I won't argue the point. But I've come all the way out here to discuss something more pressing with you."

"Why are you here?"

"I've come to speak to you regarding Terra Delarosa, your granddaughter." She paused. "I'm with Children and Family Services. Her case file has been assigned to me."

Reluctantly Cyrus opened the door wider. "Come in." He cleared the table and invited her to sit. A dishtowel was tossed over the stack of dirty pots and plates in the sink. Empty and half-drunk liquor bottles were scattered about the kitchen. Cyrus started a fresh pot of coffee. "I haven't seen Terra since she was a toddler. Her mother and I had a falling out. Is she all right?"

Roberta opened her briefcase and set papers and a manila folder on the table. "I'm still catching up on all the details. Actually, I was assigned to her case just this morning. I haven't had enough time to assess everything in detail, but there was a serious incident. It happened last night."

Cyrus poured them both cups of coffee and sat across from the woman. His mind swirled with what felt like a million separate thoughts. "What kind of incident, Ms. Johnson?"

"Please call me 'Roberta.'" She was leafing through the file papers. After a minute, she looked up. "Last night, your granddaughter, Terra, left her foster home without telling anyone. This was her fifth foster placement. She then stole a handgun off a police officer, and according to the official report I received today, it either discharged accidentally, or she fired it at him. They're not sure."

"Did the officer survive…or is he…?" Cyrus stammered as a sudden paralyzing shock overwhelmed his ability to find the right words.

"He lived," Roberta continued slowly. "Apparently the bullet shattered a walk-in display cooler near the officer. He was struck with flying shards of glass and needed to get some stitches, but otherwise he's fine. He's very shaken up, as you can imagine. They put him on four weeks administrative leave, and I suspect they'll require him to undergo psychiatric counseling."

"And, Terra, where is she? What have they done with her?"

"They found her a few blocks away in the city park a short time later. She was in the children's playground area, sleeping on a bench," Roberta said. "She isn't hurt. From what I understand, Terra dropped the gun after shooting it then ran off. When they located her, she was carried to a cruiser and slept all the way to the station. They waited until she woke up this morning to get a statement from her. She's been transferred to my department at Children and Family Services for the time being. She's safe at our temporary care facility."

Cyrus got up from the table and paced the room, trying to collect his thoughts. "What's going to happen to her now?" he asked.

"As of this moment, there's a disagreement within the police department and my office as to what exactly we should do regarding Terra…" Roberta lost her train of thought. Zeezoo, who'd been lying low in the next room ever since Cyrus answered the door, had landed in the middle of the table, seemingly flying in from out of nowhere, and startled the woman.

Anticipating her reaction to the sparrow's unexpected presence, Cyrus gave the woman an explanation before she was able to regroup. "Don't mind Zeezoo. He lives here, more or less, and has since he was a chick."

If Roberta had other questions about the bird, she didn't ask them. She recovered, continuing on in the same organized, professional manner. "Mr. Kane, this is off the record. The police are embarrassed. Their higher-ups don't want to press charges against an eight-year-old who was able to take a loaded firearm from one of their most experienced officers. I'm telling you this in confidence. Fortunately, the facts about what happened haven't reached the media. The police chief and his people would like to keep it that way and dismiss the case as an unfortunate accident."

She took a sip of coffee and went on. "To answer your question, we're not sure what to do with her. If at all possible, we'd like to avoid placing her in another foster home." Roberta shuffled several papers in front of her until she found a legal document. "Let me ask you, Mr. Kane. Were you aware that Terra's mother, your daughter Mary, was sentenced to three years in prison for drug possession and grand theft?"

"I learned about it afterward." Cyrus sat back down.

"And did you know she was granted early release from the state penitentiary six months ago?"

"No one told me." Cyrus brushed his hand against Zeezoo to quietly shoo him off the table. The bird flew to a nearby stool. "Does Terra know about this?"

"Sadly, Mary never came for Terra. And apparently, no one has had the heart to tell your granddaughter. She believes her mother is still in custody." Roberta paused again to look over the documents. "No one has seen Mary in months. She's disappeared. She hasn't shown for her mandatory meetings with her probation officer. We've looked for her but have no idea where she is."

Cyrus went to say something, but as often happens when an older thought collides with a new one, not a word or sound came out.

"We know Mary gave us a signed paper before she was incarcerated that states you are not to visit or have anything to do with Terra," Roberta continued. "I'm not going to pry as to the reasons. That's a private matter between you and your daughter. But we're running out of options. Terra has rejected foster care repeatedly, and I fear if we can't find an acceptable living arrangement soon, the courts and legal system may have no choice but to place her in a juvenile detention center."

"What are you thinking?" asked Cyrus.

"I'm overstepping my authority by even coming here." Roberta looked across the table at Cyrus. "But since her mother has vanished and you're the only other family she has, I have to consider what's best for Terra going forward." She took another sip of coffee. "Mr. Kane, you're her grandfather. I came to ask you this question: would you be willing to let Terra come live with you?"

3

The lone window in the room dispersed the setting sun's warm light and cast a rainbow that shimmered across the opposite wall. From the foldaway bed where she lay, Terra watched the colors dance and imagined the spectacle was a diamond ready to be plucked and fashioned into a fancy ring, the kind rich ladies wear.

Other than a small wooden desk, lamp, and chair, little else was in the room. At eye level on the wall next to Terra were the names of other kids who'd been brought to the county's juvenile holding room in the past. Their names were scribbled and carved randomly like graffiti. Most had been partially scrubbed away, and only a vague trace of their existence was left in the paint. But three remained bold enough to read: "Ricky," "Jennifer," and "Doodlebug." Ricky had used something sharp, maybe a pocketknife, to permanently etch his name deep into the plaster so he wouldn't be easily forgotten. And near Jennifer's name was a large heart, drawn with an arrow piercing it.

Next to Terra on the tile floor, lay a tattered green duffel bag, her father's army jacket neatly folded atop it. Inside were her clothes and a few other belongings retrieved from the foster home. Terra got up and put her hands on the heavy canvas bag, not to open it but to feel how fat it was. Its sides bulged with everything she owned in the world.

Terra went to the window, looked outside, and thought about a girl she once knew named Christy. The two had shared a bedroom at the first foster home she was placed in. Christy was three years older and treated Terra like a baby sister. She shared her dreams and included Terra in all her future plans; every escape plot and crazy adventure; the movie stardom; the mansion and cars they'd own; shopping sprees. The two girls vowed they would never be apart.

Then late one afternoon, Terra got off the school bus, walked in the house, and Christy was gone—all her stuff, everything. Terra confronted her foster parents and asked them where her best friend was, but they refused to tell her anything. Christy never came back. Terra promised herself she wouldn't cry, but she did. She wept long and hard for weeks.

Terra tried to remember her friend's smile. *What would Christy do now?* she thought. No doubt, Christy would be planning their getaway. It would be a good scheme, filled with famous people and lots of money. Terra thought about opening the glass panes, removing the screen, and jumping out, but the room she'd been confined to was on the second floor; the ground was too far away.

There was a small knock on the door. Terra heard the lock outside being turned, and Ms. Johnson came in. "Hello, dear. How are you doing?" The social worker waited for a response. When Terra didn't answer, she added, "You have a visitor."

Ms. Johnson stepped out of the room and closed the door. Terra could hear her talking to someone in a hushed voice. Less than a minute went by, and the social worker reentered. With her was an older heavy-set man with a wrinkled, unshaven face and a tangled gray mop of hair. His clothes looked scruffy. He wore dirt-stained jeans and beat-up leather boots that were badly scraped and cracked. She could smell him from across the room.

"Well, I'll leave you two alone," said Ms. Johnson. She gave a quick nod to the ragged-looking stranger and shut the door on her way out.

Without saying a word, the old man made his way to the chair by the desk and leaned against it for support. He looked out the window. "It's funny how life is, don't you think?" he said. Terra wasn't sure if he was talking to her or himself. He stared into the distance and added, "Look at it...the sunset. Is there anything in this world more alive, more majestic?"

He seemed to be lost somewhere deep in his thoughts. The last light of the day shone on his face. Terra didn't answer; she was trying her best to ignore him. Finally, after a time, he turned to her and sighed. "I know what you're thinking. Who is this ugly old man?"

"Who are you?" asked Terra.

"I'm your grandfather."

"How come I don't know you?" Terra studied the man's face closer, trying to catch some hint that he was lying or maybe find a resemblance to herself. She saw neither.

"I haven't seen you since you took your first steps and said your first words," Cyrus said calmly. "You were too young at the time to remember me. I do regret it—I mean...not finding out where you were, not getting to know you. But your mother made it clear she didn't want me in your life."

His voice was shaky. Terra noticed his hands were trembling slightly. He rested for a moment before going on. "She told me to stay away from you. She told me I'm no good...no good to anyone. She didn't like who I am...or was. It's complicated."

"You're lying. Why did you come here?" Terra felt herself suddenly being pulled in a direction she didn't want to go. She felt confused. She didn't want to know this strange man pretending to be her grandpa.

"I've been asked to take care of you." Cyrus looked nervous and, even worse, unsure of what he was saying. He stumbled over his words. "I want you to come live with me…maybe just for a while. I'm not sure really. It's whatever you want. I came here for you."

There was no hesitation in Terra's mind. "You faker! You're a liar!" she yelled. "I don't know you. I don't want to go with you. If you were really my grandpa, you would have come for me a long time ago, before they made me live in all those foster homes. I hate you! Leave me alone!" She sat back down on the foldaway bed, covered her head with both hands, and cried.

With her eyes closed tight, Terra heard his movement and felt the man's embrace. He was hugging her. "I'm truly sorry," Cyrus whispered. "I regret some things. You deserved better. I'm sorry." He let go of her.

Terra looked up. He was standing near the desk. She watched him pull an envelope or letter from inside his jacket. "Coming here and seeing you…I want you to know, Terra. You look like your mother when she was your age. And I thought my heart would burst the day she was born because I loved her so completely. Until today, she was the most wonderful thing I'd ever seen. And you…right here, right now, I feel the same way. You're so beautiful. Please believe me." With that, he laid the envelope on the desk and quietly walked out.

Terra waited for the door to close before getting up to go see what the man had left. It was a red envelope with her name handwritten on the front. She quickly opened it. Inside was a Valentine's Day card with a cartoon of a smiling skunk and a red cut-out heart over its shoulder. It read, "I might be a little 'stinker,' valentine, but—" And the skunk held a second heart-shaped valentine in its paws that said, "Be mine!" Inside the card, written in pencil, were the words, "To Terra. I love you. —Grandpa."

Roberta Johnson caught sight of Cyrus Kane as he walked through the lobby. She stopped him before he made it out the front door to ask how things had gone, but he was in no mood to answer questions. He just shook his head.

The sun had set fully. Outside Children and Family Services, the night air was beginning to feel a lot colder. There were fewer cars around the building than earlier, and one by one, the streetlights were coming on. Most of the staff had gone home for the day.

It took Cyrus a few minutes to remember where he had left his truck. By then, he had stumbled off in the wrong direction for several blocks. He retraced his steps and found it eventually, parked cockeyed on a side street. Zeezoo was perched on the steering wheel. He'd insisted on coming. "Move over," said Cyrus.

Cyrus started the truck, backed up, and began to pull away. Suddenly something in the street moved. He spotted it at the very last moment out of the corner of his eye. He slammed on the brakes. His heart raced. A small silhouette had darted in front of the truck. Cyrus got out to see what he might have hit, maybe a stray dog or cat.

There, in the middle of the road, stood Terra.

"Are you okay?" he asked.

Terra didn't answer but instead hugged him. She wouldn't let go.

4

"Get all your belongings together, Terra," Roberta said. "Your grandfather should be arriving soon."

"Yes, ma'am." Terra got up off the foldaway bed and held out her hand. "Here. I'm done with these. Thank you for letting me borrow them." She gave Roberta her fingernail clippers.

"You're welcome, dear." Smiling, she left the room and closed the door behind her.

Terra sat back down, moved aside a pillow, and took another look at her handiwork. She had carved her name deep into the wall next to the bed, using the tip of the metal nail file on Roberta's fingernail clippers. Around her name, she had carefully etched a large five-pointed star. *Now I'm famous,* she thought.

A week had passed since her grandfather's unexpected arrival back into her life, and only a day since he'd been granted temporary custody of Terra. Roberta oversaw and guided Cyrus through the process. He had to sign a thick stack of mandatory legal documents, confirming he would abide by all state and county child protection rules and regulations, before the authorities would allow Terra to move in with him. Some of the most important stipulations Cyrus agreed to were the following: Terra could be removed from his home without notice for any safety violations or for failure to protect and supervise her properly. She also could be forcibly taken if she ran away or got into trouble with the law again. Random inspections would be conducted to ensure her well-being.

With Roberta's help, Terra was enrolled in a different public school closer to the farm. She had one week off to adjust to her new surroundings before attending.

Roberta also persuaded the police not to press charges. There were several behind-closed-door meetings to discuss Terra's fate. The lead prosecutor of juvenile offenders wanted her to spend time in juvenile detention before being released. Others wanted a less severe penalty. There were heated arguments back and forth. Eventually, a compromise was reached. Since Terra was only eight years old and had no prior run-ins with the law except for having been a repeat runaway, the prosecutor overseeing the case agreed to entrust her to Children and Family Services for the time being. An open file would be kept on Terra in the event there were any further problems.

Wearing her father's army jacket, Terra waited for her grandpa in the downstairs lobby, her duffel bag by her feet. Boredom quickly set in. There was nothing to do. The morning sky outside turned dark and gloomy, and it began to rain.

She watched visitors and employees come and go. A man wearing a suit walked past and said hello. Seeing him brought back fleeting memories of another close friend she had met in foster care, a girl named Bliss. A year younger than Terra and quite small, the girl was brought one evening to Terra's second foster home with deep bruises all over her body. Terra looked after Bliss like a big sister, just as Christy had with her. The girl told stories, mostly about how her father had a real bad temper and hit her almost every day. And how her mother got beatings too.

According to Bliss, her mom wouldn't leave her dad because she was afraid of what he might do. Terra and Bliss shared the same bedroom for six or seven months. Then the girl's father showed up one Sunday, dressed in a nice tailored suit like he was heading to church, and took Bliss. Terra never saw her friend again.

Finally, her grandpa arrived. Terra was relieved and excited. He met briefly with Roberta, signed more papers, and grabbed Terra's heavy bag. He didn't have an umbrella. She ran with him through the downpour and puddles to the truck. Zeezoo was waiting inside.

"Are you hungry?" asked Cyrus.

Terra nodded. She was very hungry.

He smiled. "Do you like pancakes? We can go to the Waffle Hut. They have great pancakes and waffles. We can get whatever you want."

Terra loved pancakes, especially pancakes with lots of chocolate chips in them. "Sounds really good," she said.

Suddenly, there was an ear-piercing shriek. Terra had climbed into the truck without noticing Zeezoo. He was perched on the dash, staring back at her. Cyrus laughed. He had forgotten to tell her about the bird.

"How did this thing get in here, Grandpa?" she asked, wide-eyed and a little afraid. "Where did it come from?"

"His name is Zeezoo," Cyrus answered, as if the young sparrow's presence were perfectly normal. "He's kind of attached to me."

"Is he like a pet?" Terra asked.

"No." Cyrus glanced at his two passengers as he pulled away from the curb. "He's more like a friend." A torrent of winter rain was coming down, making it hard to see the road. The windshield wipers struggled to keep up. As the truck turned and bounced over rough spots in the road, Zeezoo kept his balance.

"Isn't he supposed to be flapping around in the wild?" Terra couldn't take her eyes off the bird. "Why does he want to stay with you?"

Cyrus thought for a moment then sighed. "He was a baby, just a chick. It was a year ago, maybe longer; I forget. He was lying on the ground by the barn. I heard him crying. He had fallen out of the nest. I could see it—the nest, I mean—high up where there's an open hole in the wood that needs to be patched." He stopped to concentrate on the wet roads before continuing.

"I got a ladder and climbed to where the nest was. But when I went to put him back, there was nothing in it, no brothers and sisters, just some loose feathers. I waited around for a mama bird to return, but I never saw her. I might have missed her. I don't know." He paused again. "So I tried to help him live. I fed him best I could and stayed with him all day and all night, for a long time—I don't know how long—until he got strong enough to not need me so much."

"Why did you name him 'Zeezoo'?" Terra studied the sparrow closely: his tiny head and beak; his brown, gray and white markings; the way his perky eyes stared back at her.

"That's a different story," said Cyrus. But he didn't tell it. They'd arrived at the Waffle Hut. Zeezoo was left alone in the truck while Terra and her grandpa ran through the rain to the restaurant.

Before ducking inside, Cyrus shouted back, "I'll bring you a banana waffle and some fries!"

Zeezoo heard him and happily chirped twice.

Maybe it was because Terra had little to call her own, or perhaps some other reason, but from the moment her grandpa parked his truck next to the farmhouse, and she saw the run-down barn and overgrown fields for the first time, she loved everything about the place.

The rain was still coming down but not as heavily. They rushed inside to dry off. Zeezoo flew to the table and waited for the promised waffle and fries. Cyrus brought him a plate filled with bits and pieces of the still-warm morsels.

Terra was given a bedroom on the second floor across from the staircase. The dusty room had once belonged to her mother when she was a girl. It hadn't been lived in for years and smelled like an antique rug.

Cyrus opened a window in the bedroom to air it out, changed the pillowcase and sheets on the bed, and brought in a heavier blanket. He also knocked down a large cobweb in the closet and emptied the dresser of old garments and forgotten knickknacks. Terra hung up her clothes and put away her belongings. Afterward, she flopped on the bed and stared up at the ceiling.

She thought, *This is the most wonderful room ever. I never want to leave.* And even though the day was still young, and there was much to see and do, her eyes closed, and she fell asleep listening to the rain's gentle lullaby.

5

Terra spent the week off from school getting to know her grandpa better and exploring the farm. Early in the morning on her first full day, she followed him to the barn, where he kept hay and oats for the horse and feed for the chickens. The two goats were let out of a small pen so they could eat grass in a nearby field.

The mare's name was Lizzie. Cyrus didn't know her exact age, but he reckoned she was close to thirty years old. She was an American Quarter Horse, chestnut in color, with a black mane and tail. On a neighboring farm, she'd accidentally stepped in a groundhog hole, which fractured her lower leg. The owners were going to put her down when, at the last minute, Cyrus heard the news and offered to take the injured horse off their hands. Lizzie never healed properly and walked with a distinct limp, but she was no longer in pain. She hobbled around and spent most of her days quietly resting.

Inside the barn were stalls and a hayloft. There were horse blankets, a wagon, wheelbarrow, ladder, pitchfork, shovel, all kinds of tools for fixing things, and implements for planting and harvesting out in the field. There were cutting tools, spades, a posthole digger, and rolls of chicken wire too.

Cyrus gave Terra a few simple safety rules to follow; she wasn't allowed to climb up into the hayloft and wasn't allowed to get into the stall with Lizzie alone. She wasn't allowed to play with the stored tools and farm equipment. Terra could wander by herself pretty much wherever she liked as long as the farmhouse and barn were in sight. Cyrus didn't want her going beyond the fields to the woods nearby or anywhere by the creek that marked the property's southern boundary.

Terra was introduced to the three hens on the farm: Eeny, Meeny, and Miny. There had once been a Moe, but the fourth hen hadn't been seen for two months. Her recent disappearance remained a mystery, though Edgar was strongly suspected as having played a part. Cyrus searched all over for Moe; he investigated the chicken coop and surrounding area for fox and coyote footprints but couldn't find any evidence of foul play.

The two billy goats lived in a separate pen, where they had a small open shelter they could sleep under at night. They both wore little beards and had similar white-and-tan markings. Neither had a name, and Terra's grandpa referred to them simply as "the brothers." Whenever the goats spotted Terra outside, they trotted over to the fence line to entice her to come closer. They'd aggressively push their faces against her hands to get her to scratch their necks and heads, and they especially liked to be rubbed between their horns.

Terra asked her grandpa if she could give each goat a name, and he said yes. But she wasn't sure what to call them just yet and decided to take her time so their new names would be good ones.

Once the animals were fed, Cyrus almost always went back into the house to sip on a pint of whiskey, leaving Terra to play and wander free outdoors. She explored the barn, careful not to touch the things her grandpa had told her to avoid. She sat on the rusted, broken tractor and pretended she was driving it and plowing. She went out into the wide fields, overgrown with scruffy weeds, and imagined they were filled again with long rows of tall corn and wheat, all the different crops her grandpa had said he and the Kane family used to grow there.

By afternoon, Cyrus was usually a little tipsy from drinking. But unlike some who get mean after having a few drinks, he'd sit down on his recliner and doze off. When he awakened from his nap, he was better for a while. Then he'd start sipping whiskey again. Terra could see her grandpa had a good heart and cared about others, but his life was like a Ferris wheel spinning round and round. It never went anywhere.

During those first days on the farm, Zeezoo captured much of Terra's attention. She liked watching the sparrow's strange and funny relationship with her grandpa. By midday, Zeezoo often disappeared, but he always returned. Terra spent hours scouting for him and spying on his every move. She saw him sometimes in the distance, flitting about near the woods or perched high atop the barn, detached and seemingly indifferent to everyone and everything around him. But if her grandpa started the truck to go somewhere, or if he whistled, Zeezoo would magically appear, ready to go for a ride and follow the old man wherever he went.

He must think he's a dog, Terra thought.

One morning, Terra was closely watching the hens. She'd just finished helping her grandpa gather three eggs, toss grain in the pen, and fill their bowl with tasty mealworms, when Zeezoo swooped past her head with what looked like a long piece of straw hanging from his beak. He landed on top of the chicken coop and rested there for a moment before hurriedly flying off across a field. She lost sight of him when he reached the woods.

Terra asked her grandpa, "Do birds eat straw?"

"No." Cyrus was puzzled by the question. He hadn't looked up from what he was doing and didn't know Zeezoo had come and gone. "Why are you asking?"

"Then why does Zeezoo have straw in his mouth?"

Cyrus wiped his hands on his shirt and shut the lattice gate to the coop behind him. "Well, the air is a little warmer," he answered. "He must be ready."

"Ready for what?" asked Terra.

"To build a nest," her grandpa answered with a smile. "It's time."

Terra didn't understand. She knew birds made nests to lay their eggs in, of course, but she couldn't figure out why Zeezoo might want to build one. He was a boy after all, and seemed too tame. It didn't make sense. As they walked back to the house, she wondered about the nest.

"Why is it time now?" she asked.

Cyrus sat down on the wooden steps that led into the farmhouse. Terra sat beside him. "It's like this," he explained. "Zeezoo is a wild thing, and inside him is a nature he can't help feeling. He was born with an inner mechanism or clock that tells him what to do."

He looked over at his granddaughter, who was listening carefully. "When the skies start to warm," he continued, "the clock rings an alarm inside a boy sparrow like Zeezoo, telling him it's time to find a mate and raise a family. So he goes off and starts to build a nest, hoping he can attract some pretty girl sparrow to it. He starts building the nest, and then the girl comes along and helps him finish it."

"How does the girl know he's making a nest?"

"The boy sparrow flies all around looking for a girl sparrow, and if he finds one he likes, he starts courting her, chirping and singing and acting like a fool. He tries to get the girl to follow him so he can show her the nice nest he started."

"Then what?" asked Terra.

"The girl has to decide whether she likes him and the nest he's making. And she might get a better offer from another boy sparrow down the road. If she refuses to stay, then he moves on. He has to start over and find someone new to court."

"What if she likes him?"

"Then, she stays with the boy and helps him finish the nest, so it's nice and comfortable," her grandpa said. He was looking up at the sky at something, maybe nothing. "Sparrows usually stay together for life."

Terra liked the idea of Zeezoo finding and courting a girl sparrow and the two of them loving each other for life. Her grandpa didn't say "love," but what else could it be? It sounded exciting.

"Can we go look at the nest?" she asked. "I want to see it."

"I don't think we should." Cyrus stood up to go in the house. "If we get near the nest while he's trying to build it, there's a chance we could mess things up. Zeezoo might stop what he's doing or lose out on finding a girl because we got in the way. It's better if we give him some space right now." He opened the door to go inside the house. "Do you understand?" he asked.

"Yes," she answered. But Terra hadn't promised to stay away from the nest. She was excited and eager to see what the nest looked like. She thought, *Zeezoo won't mind as long as I don't get too close or try to touch it.*

Terra lingered outside the farmhouse, peeking through the window every so often. As soon as her grandpa sat in the recliner, put his feet up, and closed his eyes, she set out for the woods on the far side of the field to where she had last seen Zeezoo.

It was a long walk across the rough overgrown field, a lot further than she'd first thought. The ground was full of tall weeds and uneven from decades of plowing. She nearly fell down several times tripping on large unseen dirt clumps and prickly vines. Sand burrs were sticking to her shoelaces. By the time she reached the edge of the woods, she had almost forgotten why she had come.

Close up, the woods looked much different than they did earlier from a distance. They covered many acres of land along the backside of the farm and were several miles deep. There was a vast chaotic tangle of underbrush mixed with different kinds of trees. The dense canopy of limbs and leaves cast everything below in shadows.

Hesitant to step into the woods alone, Terra waited several minutes for Zeezoo to appear. She walked along the edge of the woods, checking the nearest treetops for a nest and looking for open places where he might have flown, but there was no sign of him.

After a while, she got tired and gave up searching. The sparrow could be most anywhere. The woods were too big and spooky, and he was too small. She didn't want to risk getting lost. Besides, she felt thirsty. *Maybe I'll try again tomorrow*, she thought. Terra turned to leave then paused. She heard something faint that sounded like soft chirping, muffled and faraway. It was there for a moment but had stopped. She stood still and listened. A minute or so later, she heard it again.

The chirping was definitely coming from the woods, somewhere to the right. It fell silent, and then another quick chirp echoed again, and a minute later again. Terra walked toward the sound, trying to follow it to its source, until she could go no further. Whoever was doing the chirping lay hidden just beyond a bushy area of the woods with no ready-made path into it.

It might have been a different bird, but Terra was certain the call had come from Zeezoo. Over the past few days, she had heard him chirping a number of times, mostly in response to her grandpa, and she recognized his voice. Then she heard a rustling and saw a flash of something fly between the bushes and leaves a few feet away from her in the woods. She pushed apart a couple of low-lying branches and carefully made her way through a narrow passage of thick bushes until she reached a small clearing.

Seconds later, Terra heard something move overhead. She glanced up, and there on a limb, about halfway up a big pine tree, was Zeezoo. He had a twig in his beak. He looked right at her before flying over to a large gaping hole on the tree's trunk. She watched him place the twig in the hole and poke at it. Then he flew off quickly. She waited for him to return. And he did, minutes later, with another long piece of straw or a twig. He again went to the hole's entrance and positioned it inside. Terra was thrilled. Her grandpa had been right about Zeezoo and the nest.

Terra kept her promise about not getting too close to Zeezoo. From below she watched him come and go with all sizes of twigs and straw. He worked steadily at building the nest for more than an hour, but eventually he flew off and didn't return.

When Terra came out of the woods, she took off one of her socks and tied it to a bush at the edge of the field to mark the hidden entry path to the nest. Then she ran, skipped, and sang "Old MacDonald Had a Farm" all the way back to the farmhouse.

6

With each passing day, Zeezoo became more and more attached to Terra. In the morning, if the door was open to her bedroom, he'd fly in to see if she was awake. If her eyes were closed, he'd land on her head and gently tug at her hair. At the table, he perched next to her and patiently waited for her to pass bits of her bread and potato to him. Whenever she explored the world outdoors, he called to her and closely watched where she went and what she was doing.

Zeezoo knew he could trust Terra to keep the location of the nest a secret. He worked a few hours every day to make the nest bigger while she sometimes watched from below. She even brought handfuls of straw from the barn so he wouldn't have to fly far for more. He liked to weave short lengths of straw together with dry grass from the field and broken twigs from the woods.

The nest lay in a fairly deep, good-sized hole that had been carved out by a woodpecker many years before. It was halfway up a mature pine, not too far into the dense woods. For a young family of sparrows, it was an ideal location. From a nearby branch, Zeezoo would be able to look out in all directions for predators. He also could see the farm-house and barn in the distance.

One cloudy afternoon, when they were alone together in the woods, Terra asked Zeezoo, "Do you know what kind of girlfriend you want?"

Zeezoo had just worked a particularly large twig into the hole to brace the front of the nest, and was taking a short break. He looked down and chirped two times.

"You probably want a girl who's really pretty," added Terra. "But you know beauty is only skin deep, right?"

Zeezoo cocked his head inquisitively and listened. He had his own natural inherited sense of who the right girl would be and what to do if he met her, but he liked Terra's opinions on things and was anxious to hear what she had to say.

"You need to find somebody who's nice," said Terra. She picked up a piece of straw off a little pile she had brought him and wagged it in the air. Zeezoo landed on her wrist and plucked it from her. He then flew back to the nest.

Terra had lots of useful information and ideas about romance and relationships that she wanted to share. It came pouring out of her. "Zeezoo, the person you marry has to be smart, and they've got to be funny too. I like boys who make me laugh."

When Zeezoo finished with one piece of straw, she held up anoth-er. He retrieved them one by one. Terra went on. "You need to be care-ful, Zeezoo, 'cause some girls look pretty, but when you get to know them, you find out they only care about their own feelings. Girls can be mean. Some will tell lies right to your face. And it's okay if the person you like doesn't have much," she added, "because having nice things doesn't make you honest or someone worth believing in. Trust me,

Zeezoo. This is important stuff. You'll want to find a girl who's good on the inside, like you."

Before she could say more, the skies darkened, and a torrent of cold rain poured down. Terra yelled, "Bye!" and raced out of the woods and across the open field to the farmhouse. For the next few minutes, Zeezoo could hear her shrieking, "Eek! Eek!"

Zeezoo fluffed his feathers and bathed in the short-lived downpour before taking refuge in the hole, atop the nest. With about a fourth of the nest in place, the time had come to find a mate to help him finish it. But he wasn't sure where to look.

Around the farm, he hadn't seen any birds that looked like him. There had been a hawk, as well as several crows, robins, bluebirds and cardinals. There had even been a rather talkative herring gull who had stopped by unexpectedly one day, asking for directions to the sea; he was lost, but not another sparrow.

Since he knew most every square inch of the farm by heart, there seemed little chance he'd ever find a mate unless he widened his search. Zeezoo tried to think of where to start looking. Close to the farm, the only place he hadn't explored was the shallow creek nearby. So he decided to try there first.

Trees, low bushes, and overgrown grass extended along both sides of the creek. Its waters either trickled or raced along, depending on the time of year. Since it was late winter and the air had warmed a few degrees, the creek had begun to rise. Its chilled flow cascaded over and around the innumerable rocks, massive and small, that littered its entire length. In certain places, one could still jump from rock to rock in order to reach the other side. In a few short weeks, however, the steadily rising water would submerge all but the largest rocks. It would soon be more difficult to traverse from one side to the other without getting wet.

Zeezoo surveyed the creek from above, flying back and forth both upstream and downstream several times, before settling on a willow that overlooked the water.

He observed the world around him and began to sing. His voice rose above the gentle rustling of the leaves and the gurgling of the water. He sang loudly. He sang softly. He got into a rhythm and experimented with fresh combinations of pleasing sounds. His melodies echoed and flowed like the creek below.

If the right girl is listening, thought Zeezoo, *she'll answer me in time.*

He put his heart and soul into his songs and went on and on, until he heard a rustling in the tall grass nearby.

Curious, Zeezoo stopped singing to swoop down and see what was moving. He landed on a flat rock next to the creek, but before he could raise his head or take a step, something knocked him down hard onto his back. In the next instant, he felt a paw on his chest and sharp teeth around his neck.

"Don't eat me!" screamed Zeezoo.

The mouth around his throat released its grip, but the heavy paw wouldn't let him up. "Shut your yap, bird! You're mine now!"

Zeezoo looked up at the face of his attacker. It was a large raccoon, its teeth bared. "What do you want?" he asked in a panicked and high, squeaky voice. "Are you going to eat me?"

"Eat you?" answered the raccoon. "No way! First, we're going to rough you up! And then we're going to break your wings! Then, we're going to send you packing back to your little friends as a warning."

"Who is 'we'?" Zeezoo asked, trying to choke back his fear. On the one hand, he felt relieved he wouldn't be eaten, but having his bones broken meant certain death too. A little sparrow unable to fly in the wild wouldn't survive for long.

"We is us!" The answer came from somewhere in the tall grass. Zeezoo turned his head to see who and what it was that had spoken, and out slithered a rat snake.

"Allow me to introduce myself," said the snake. "I go by many names, but most around here call me Shorty. And my loyal associate here, whom you've met, is Angel."

With the raccoon's paw still on his chest, Zeezoo could barely breathe. "Please don't hurt me!" he begged, gasping for air.

The snake slithered closer until its face caressed Zeezoo's cheek. "This is your lucky day, kid, 'cause although Angel and I were born to consume the tasty flesh of other creatures such as yourself, we've decided to reject the savage habits of our forefathers."

"Yeah, count yourself lucky, bird," said Angel. "We don't eat anything that has a face. We're what you call strict vegetarians."

Shorty flicked his forked tongue across Zeezoo's head. "But unlucky for you, friend, you're trespassing on our turf." He circled around Zeezoo. "Who sent you? Was it those crows? We had an agreement."

"I don't know any crows. Please believe me."

"Then why are you here?" asked Angel. "And who are you?" He eased the pressure on Zeezoo's chest but continued to hold him captive beneath his paw.

"I just wanted to sing…here by the creek. That's all. My name is Zeezoo."

An odd smile swept over Shorty's face. "Ah, I see. You're a lover." He laughed. "Let me ask you…by chance, would you be singing for a girl?"

"Yes, but I haven't met her yet."

"Ha-ha-ha. Now we have an understanding," said Shorty. "Angel and I here are also lovers. By nature, all creatures are lovers. Well, at least some of the time we are, when we aren't hunting and eating each other."

"Where did you come from?" Angel asked Zeezoo.

"I grew up right over there." Zeezoo motioned a wing in the direction of the farm. "I've lived outside these woods all my life."

"Yes…yes, now I see," said Shorty. "You came here with an innocent spirit, and your purpose is part of your nature, which means it's mostly pure." He glanced up at the sky before turning his attention back to Zeezoo. "You're small and pose no danger to us. This is clear."

"What are we going to do, boss?" asked Angel.

"Hmm, let me think," said Shorty. "This bird may be of some use to us."

"I'll do whatever you want," said Zeezoo. "I promise not to cause trouble, but please don't hurt me."

Shorty circled Zeezoo and flicked his tongue several times. After a minute or two, he stopped. "Here is how you're going to save yourself," he said. "We could use someone on our side who is able to fly, somebody who can scout the territory and keep an eye out from above." He again brought his face close to Zeezoo's. "I want you to join our organization. If you agree to join us, we will spare your life, and in the future, you may come and go as you wish."

"What exactly do you want me to do?" asked Zeezoo.

"You'll agree to keep a lookout for predators. You'll protect us when called upon, and in return, we'll protect you," said Shorty. "We need to know you're on our side."

"But I'm not on anybody's side," said Zeezoo.

"Aw, my poor bird, but everybody has to pick a side," said Shorty. "It's just the way things are. You're either with us or against us. Which is it?"

Zeezoo didn't understand exactly what choosing sides meant, but he was in no position to ask questions. "I'm on your side," he peeped.

"Excellent!" said Shorty, smiling. "Angel, let this bird up, and apologize to him."

Angel took his paw off Zeezoo's chest and lifted him to his feet. "Please accept my apology, Mr. Zeezoo. Are you okay?"

Still reeling from the unexpected assault, Zeezoo didn't move a muscle. Angel brushed a bit of dry earth off Zeezoo's feathers and patted him on the head.

"I think so," answered Zeezoo.

"Welcome, brother!" said Shorty. "I apologize most profusely for not being more gracious, but around here, one must always be cautious." He slithered close to Zeezoo and lightly kissed him on both cheeks.

"But that's in the past, isn't it? We're now brothers!" added Shorty. "It's a glorious thing. We'll help and protect you, and in return, you'll help and protect us."

"So are we friends?" asked Zeezoo.

"Yes, brother! Yes!" said Shorty. "From this point forward, for as long as we have breath, we'll be the best of friends."

Zeezoo liked what he heard and agreed to be a part of the small brotherhood. Angel and Shorty continued to apologize. And together they worked out a simple plan that would benefit all three.

7

It was Monday, time to go back to school. The week before, Ms. Johnson at Children and Family Services made final arrangements to have
Terra transferred and enrolled in her new school, and Cyrus took her to
buy some new clothes. She had worn out or outgrown most of what she
owned. He made sure they bought a couple pairs of jeans for around the
farm, but otherwise, he let his granddaughter pick out what she wanted.

"Hurry up!" yelled Cyrus. "You'll miss the bus!"

Perched on a faucet, Zeezoo watched Terra fret over and fix her
hair in the bathroom mirror. She couldn't make up her mind. First she
put it in a tight ponytail. She stared at herself, frowned, and undid the
band, fluffed it all loose, and frowned again.

"Coming!" said Terra. She placed two purple barrettes in her hair
to hold it in place, smiled, and ran out.

"Don't forget your backpack," said Cyrus.

An early-morning fog blanketed the world outside as they hurried
along the dirt road to the main highway.

Zeezoo came to see Terra off. For several days, he had heard Cyrus
and Terra discuss something called school, and he was curious. Their

conversations made school sound like it was two different places. School for Terra was simply a place to meet new friends. But her grandpa had strong opinions that it was something else. He said school was where the seeds of greatness grew, a place of opportunity not to be squandered. He told her to pay attention in class and to study.

Zeezoo flew to a nearby fencepost and waited. *Maybe school is all kinds of things*, he thought.

Soon, the bright flashing lights and silhouette of a large yellow bus pierced the dense fog. It slowed to a stop and extended a crossing arm. Its doors opened.

Terra gave her grandpa a hug and said, "Goodbye, Zeezoo."

Cyrus and Zeezoo watched her step onto the bus and find an empty seat. Terra waved to them from a window as the bus lurched forward and disappeared into the mist.

Back at the farmhouse, they came across Edgar pacing at the front door. When the cat saw them, he whined noisily to be let in. Being nocturnal, he'd been out roaming all night and wanted his breakfast. Cyrus filled a dish with milk and another with leftover chicken and set them on the floor.

From atop the table, Zeezoo kept an eye on the cat. Cyrus went outside to feed the animals. When he returned, he emptied the kitchen sink of dirty plates, glasses, and pots, then washed and dried everything. He cleaned the counter and stove before reaching into a cupboard for a nearly empty bottle of whiskey.

Cyrus sat at the table, uncapped the large bottle, and slugged down what little was left. He wiped his mouth on his sleeve and carelessly let the bottle drop to the floor. It shattered, sending shards of glass flying. Edgar leapt and ran out of the room.

"We need to take a trip into town, Zeezoo," said Cyrus. His eyes were bloodshot, his hands trembling.

Zeezoo didn't move and said nothing.

By the time they reached town, the fog had lifted. The sky emerged bluer than it had in months. Cyrus drove fifteen miles to the nearest liquor store to buy more whiskey, but he arrived much too early. The place wasn't yet open; their lights were off. He parked, walked over, and took a look at the business-hours sign on the door. "Damn it," he muttered. It would be another two hours before they opened.

Across from the liquor store, in the same plaza, was Piggles, the local-owned grocery chain. Cyrus decided to go in and buy a fresh loaf of bread, mac and cheese, frozen pizza, and a few other essentials he knew his granddaughter liked. Zeezoo waited for him in the truck, its windows left open partway to let in fresh air.

Thirty minutes or so later, Cyrus returned, his arms loaded down with plastic bags. He tossed them in the back and headed to the feed store to kill more time. He needed oats for Lizzie and pellets for the chickens.

On the way, some two or three miles up the road, they came upon a line of traffic cones and a work zone flagger, wearing a yellow hardhat and a reflective safety vest. The flagger, who was holding up a pole with a two-sided STOP/SLOW sign atop it, raised her hand for Cyrus to stop.

Just ahead, a road crew was busy adding a new turn lane and widening a section of the street that ran alongside one of the last parcels of woods and pastureland within the city limits. The land, once owned by an old rancher who Cyrus knew well, had been sold at auction, and was in the process of being cleared by a team of construction workers, using an excavator and other heavy earth-moving equipment.

Cyrus stopped to allow a bulldozer to cross the street.

"See that, Zeezoo. Another worthless real estate development project," Cyrus grumbled. "I don't see the point of it all. Do you?"

Zeezoo was perched on the dash, watching the road crew. He didn't understand what Cyrus was trying to say, but chirped once anyway in agreement.

"I mean, why can't the corporations and investors behind these projects just leave well enough alone? They're quick to plow under the old and tear down the past, always eager to call it progress. And do things get better? No! The world doesn't change."

The flagger turned her sign to SLOW and motioned for Cyrus to move.

"I'm sure the greedy fools who bought the land aren't even from around here."

There had been a time when Cyrus could easily drive from one end of town to the other in the blink of an eye, but no longer. Urban sprawl had steadily taken root over the years, and depending on the day of the week and traffic congestion, the same route now took twenty-five to forty minutes. Nearly everywhere, one could still find remnants of the city's agricultural beginnings while traversing its hodgepodge of shopping districts, commercial areas, and older neighborhoods, but in truth, crop production and livestock had ceased being the local economy's main source of jobs and income many decades ago.

Another mile or two farther on, Cyrus stopped briefly at a red light. When it turned green, he glanced over and saw five or six sparrows pecking the sidewalk around a bus bench. He smiled. Zeezoo spotted them too.

The car behind them honked.

Cyrus turned right at the light and pulled over next to the curb. "Well, Zeezoo, what do you want to do?" he asked.

Zeezoo hopped up onto his shoulder and pecked him softly on the cheek. Cyrus glanced again at the sparrows scavenging for scraps near the bench and sighed.

"Do you know the way back home?"

Zeezoo chirped twice.

"Are you sure? Home is a long, long way from here. I don't want to lose you."

Zeezoo fluttered to the window, looked back at Cyrus, and chirped twice more.

"Okay," said Cyrus. "I understand. Good luck."

Catching a light breeze, Zeezoo flew off toward where the other sparrows were loosely gathered on the sidewalk. He settled atop the bench.

Cyrus' truck made a U-turn and slowly drove away.

8

Zeezoo began to sing.

The half dozen sparrows on the sidewalk were randomly rummaging through specks of debris scattered around the bench. One picked up a cigarette butt and tossed it aside. Two others were tussling over a tortilla chip. They paid no attention to him.

An elderly woman in an overcoat and holding a large purse approached. She sat down on the bench, causing a commotion. The gathering of sparrows flew off and separated, then one by one they came back to the sidewalk.

Zeezoo never moved. Perched next to the woman, he kept singing.

"Oh my, aren't you a noisy one?" said the woman.

After two or three minutes, a city bus stopped in front of the bench. Several people stepped off. The woman with the purse dug out a handful of coins and got on.

Three boy and three girl sparrows were moving about. Like Zeezoo, the boys had gray heads, white cheeks, and a black-feathered bib under their beaks. The girls were mostly dusty brown in color with no bibs.

Keeping his distance, Zeezoo studied everything the other sparrows were doing. They hopped around and pecked at the sidewalk until the little scraps of food were exhausted. When five of the six flew away and didn't return, he stayed where he was and watched the one boy sparrow who remained behind. Soon, the boy too fluttered off in the direction of several taller buildings nearby. Zeezoo decided to follow him.

The sparrow raced above the traffic and past several trees. He came to rest on a third-floor windowsill that overlooked an alleyway. Below was a dumpster filled to overflowing. Several garbage bags were piled in front of it. Zeezoo set down on a roof ledge directly across the alley from the bird.

After surveying the offerings below, the sparrow flew down and pecked the ground around the bags. He looked up. "Why are you following me?" he asked.

"I apologize," said Zeezoo. "It's just...I've never seen someone who looks like me." He flew down and landed next to the sparrow.

"You're not from around here, are you?" said the sparrow.

Attracted to the garbage, a parade of ants had formed a long line from the edge of a building to the bags. The sparrow grabbed an ant with his beak and swallowed it. Then a second one. The other ants never stopped marching.

"What do they call you?" asked Zeezoo.

The sparrow had another ant in his mouth. He gulped it down before answering. "Because I was the last of five eggs in the nest to hatch, my mom called me 'Fifth.' But my dad named me 'Little Ace,' because I can fly really good. I'm the best." He paused to look at Zeezoo. "You can call me 'Ace.' Everybody does." He cocked his head before snatching another parading ant. "And who are you?"

"Zeezoo," he answered. "I lost my mom when I was a baby, and I don't know my dad."

"That's too bad," said Ace. "Say, are you hungry? You should dig in."

"No, thanks," said Zeezoo. He had tasted mosquitoes, gnats, and a few other flying insects, but not ants. They didn't look very appetizing.

As the line of ants kept coming, Ace continued to gorge. The dumpster and garbage bags smelled of rotting meat, fruits, and vegetables. Zeezoo disliked the foul odors, but they didn't seem to bother Ace.

"You never know what you'll find lying around in a place like this," said Ace. "Last week, they forgot to close the lids on the trash bins. It was a buffet."

Zeezoo stood to the side and watched.

When Ace finished, he let out a loud burp. "Excuse me!" he said, laughing. "Ants make me gassy."

"What are you going to do now?" asked Zeezoo.

"Not sure, but I'm thinking about checking out the action at Tasty Burger. If you can keep up, you're welcome to tag along."

Before Zeezoo could say anything, Ace took off and shot straight up into the sky like a rocket, rising higher and higher. When it seemed he'd disappear right into space, he went into a dizzying free fall, and then at the last possible moment, he caught himself.

"Come on!" yelled Ace. He soared away, high above the buildings and trees, doing amazing loops and barrel rolls.

Zeezoo raced after Ace, but it was impossible to catch up. Ace was lightning fast. They flew several miles across town, until at last Ace dived and gently landed in a parking lot. Breathing hard, Zeezoo set down beside him.

"So what do you think?" asked Ace, grinning.

"Wow!" said Zeezoo, still out of breath. "I've never seen anyone fly like that."

"I know." Ace fluffed his feathers and shook his body to get rid of any residual dust from the flight. "And there's no one as good as me. Not around here, anyway."

"Where are we?" asked Zeezoo.

They were standing in the middle of a huge parking lot that surrounded a large rectangular structure on all sides. Zeezoo was puzzled; there were no cars around, not a one anywhere.

"My dad said this place is called the mall, but no one comes here anymore. They closed it. That's all I know," said Ace. "I like the parking lot 'cause it's a great place to practice taking off and landing." He pointed his wing and added, "Over there across the street is Tasty Burger. It's one of my favorite hangouts."

While Ace practiced several new flight maneuvers in the sky above the mall parking lot, Zeezoo watched car after car turn into Tasty Burger; the cars followed each other single file through the drive-through lane in much the same way as the ants had done earlier. A congregation of birds milled about outside the restaurant.

Anxious to get a closer look, Zeezoo flew across the street and landed atop a red picnic table in front of Tasty Burger. A minute or so later, Ace joined him.

The air was thick with the smells of burgers and fries. At the drive-up and inside, a lunch crowd was starting to grow. People were going inside empty-handed and coming out with bags of food. Occasionally someone tossed a tasty fry or hunk of bread to the birds, which almost always led to a squabble over the morsel. And nearly always, the larger or more aggressive bird won out over their weaker opponent.

Zeezoo, of course, was more interested in the ladies than he was the food. He watched the grayish buff-colored female sparrows flit about. Several were striking up conversations with one boy or another, then flying off, but mostly the girls kept to themselves in small groups of three or four.

Hungry again after his hard workout, Ace nabbed a tossed bit of bread roll before it hit the ground. No one had a chance to challenge him for it. Zeezoo realized speed had certain advantages in these surroundings.

"Ace, have you built a nest?" asked Zeezoo.

"Me?" Ace laughed. "No way! You won't find me grubbing away on some dinky nest and settling down. Why? Are you making a nest?"

Before Zeezoo could answer, three girls landed on the table next to them. They huddled together and began to whisper. Soon the girls raised their heads and came a little closer, standing shoulder to shoulder.

"So, Ace, tell us. Who's your friend?" said the one in the middle.

"This here is Zeezoo. Why do you want to know?" said Ace, smiling. He gave Zeezoo a wink.

"Oh…no reason," said the middle one. The three girls huddled up again and burst into giggles.

Ace leaned his head closer to Zeezoo. "Those three are sisters," he said under his breath. "They're always acting stupid. Don't pay any attention to them."

Zeezoo, however, didn't hear the last part of what Ace had said. Mesmerized by the girls already, he was only half listening; the sisters had his undivided attention. Their markings and coloration were nearly identical, making it difficult to tell them apart. Except one of the three girls was slightly smaller than the other two.

"What are your names?" asked Zeezoo.

"Oh, no!" said Ace. "Were you not listening?"

The two larger sisters perked up their heads and answered at the same time.

"Well…I'm Amelia."

"I'm Bessie."

Both fluffed their feathers and smiled.

"And I'm Elin," said the smaller one. Her voice was softer and shier than her two siblings. And unlike her sisters, she didn't smile or look Zeezoo in the eyes when she spoke. Her attention seemed to be elsewhere.

"Where do you live, Zeezoo?" asked Amelia. "Why haven't we seen you before?"

"I grew up outside of town, on a farm," said Zeezoo, puffing his chest. "That's where I'm building a nest."

The girls giggled.

"I came to look around and find a—" But before Zeezoo could say another word, a larger tough-looking male sparrow landed on the table between the girls and him.

"What do we have here?" asked the bullish sparrow in an irritated tone, interrupting the conversation.

"We're not doing anything, Thorn," said Ace. He nudged Zeezoo in the side.

Thorn hopped closer and put his beak up to Zeezoo's. "You know the rules, Ace," said Thorn. "Outsiders are forbidden here. It's locals only. So if you know what's good for you, you'll leave right now and take your new friend with you!"

"We understand, Thorn," said Ace. "My friend didn't mean any harm. He doesn't know the rules. We were just leaving, weren't we?" He nudged Zeezoo.

"No," said Zeezoo.

"What did you say?" said Thorn, shoving Zeezoo backward.

"Clean your ears," said Zeezoo. "I said I'm not going anywhere."

Thorn struck Zeezoo on the side of the head with his wing, then went to shove him again, but this time Zeezoo was ready. He leapt straight in the air, avoiding the punch, then spun in midair and landed a flying dropkick in Thorn's back, shoving the bully onto his face.

The girls gasped. Ace backed away so as not to get involved. Thorn picked himself up and whistled. Three of his buddies quickly flew in and grabbed Zeezoo by his wings. He struggled to break free but couldn't. They held on to him tightly.

Thorn again brought his beak close to Zeezoo's. "You think you're tough, don't you?" he said with a sneer. He backhanded Zeezoo's face and angrily jabbed him in the stomach.

Unable to catch his breath after Thorn's blow, Zeezoo slumped over. He tried to resist his captors but lost his strength.

Thorn struck him in the face again. "Are you ready to leave now?" he asked.

"No," said Zeezoo in a whisper, still straining to breathe. "I'm not afraid of you. I have as much right to be here as anyone."

Thorn raised his wing and thrust it forward with unrestrained fury, but the vicious blow was suddenly blocked. Elin had a tentative grip on Thorn's wing and was now standing between him and Zeezoo.

"No more!" yelled Elin. "Leave him alone."

Unsure what to do next, Thorn glared at Elin and shook her off his wing.

Elin turned to Zeezoo and put her wings around him. She whispered in his ear, "Please go. I don't want to see you hurt this way." She smacked one of the sparrows holding Zeezoo in the head. "Let go of him," she said. They did what she asked.

Zeezoo stood there, a little stunned, looking at Elin. "Thank you," he said.

"Now go!" said Elin. "Please, far from here."

Zeezoo fluffed his feathers and flew off. The sky was clear. He had nowhere to go except home, but he needed to rest for a while before attempting the long flight. The unexpected confrontation at Tasty Burger and strange emotions running wild inside him left him feeling a bit confused. He set down a few blocks away on a traffic light that overlooked a busy intersection.

He watched the people below, driving their cars, slow to a crawl, turn right and left, accelerate, and continue on in all directions. There seemed to be no end to the movements. One or more would come to a stop. And several others sped away. *To where?* he wondered.

There were so many questions he wanted to ask and too few answers. What one sees lying on the surface isn't enough to judge anything by. The world he found himself in often left him feeling kind of empty inside. Zeezoo longed to know more and understand.

These odd thoughts and others were swirling within him when he heard something in the distance, a lovely ringing sound he'd never encountered before. Bright and melodic, it seemed to be coming from somewhere beyond a line of trees nearby. Curious to see who or what could make such a noise, Zeezoo decided to fly toward it.

The spirited ringing grew ever louder, and he soon found its source in the bell tower of a church. He came to rest outside the belfry, where the tolling of the bells continued for several more minutes. When the ringing ceased, he waited and listened for it to return, but it didn't.

Zeezoo looked out across the surrounding rooftops and skyline before him, hesitant to leave. The sound of the bells had felt reassuring. An old nest lay tucked in a back corner of the belfry. Abandoned and deteriorating, it reminded Zeezoo of the farm; his mother and father, lost before he even knew them and gone forever; Cyrus and Terra; and his own nest in the woods. For the first time, he felt small and alone.

In this lofty space, close to the hushed bells, he shut his eyes and began to sing. The sad tune flowed out like a beautiful stream, unplanned, mournful, and blue. Zeezoo heard his song echo and soar gently into some middle distance amid his dreams.

When he opened his eyes, Elin was perched beside him.

9

"Zeezoo's back!" shouted Terra, running to the house. "Zeezoo came back!"

Cyrus put down his drink and stepped outside to greet his granddaughter. "Where is he?"

It had been four days since Cyrus left Zeezoo to fend for himself in town. He hadn't confessed the truth to Terra that he had let the young sparrow go off on his own. When she invariably asked him if he had seen Zeezoo anywhere, he told her no and pretended not to have a clue as to where the bird might have gone. Every day after school, Terra searched the farm and woods around the nest for the sparrow, and each time she returned with her arms folded and head hung low.

"He's over by the woods!" said Terra, bouncing with excitement. "And someone's with him."

"Show me," said Cyrus.

The two crossed the field with Terra leading the way. The weeds in the untended field had grown taller. More familiar now with the uneven ground, she effortlessly weaved around and skipped over the roughest patches. Several times Cyrus stepped into an unseen furrow and stumbled.

"Come on, Grandpa!" said Terra.

Forgetting what she'd been told about never straying into the woods, Terra brought her grandpa to its edge and led him by the hand through the dense underbrush to the pine tree. Cyrus heard chirping and looked up. There on a branch near the nest was Zeezoo. And at the entry to the nest was a female sparrow, Elin.

"Oh my," whispered Cyrus, trying not to disturb the two birds. "Will you look at that?"

Busy at work on the nest, Zeezoo didn't notice them for a few minutes. When he finally did, he chirped excitedly and hurried down to greet them both. Cyrus and Terra each received loving pecks on the cheek.

Elin kept her distance in the tree. After saying hello, Zeezoo quickly flew back to be near her. As the two sparrows worked on the nest, Cyrus and Terra watched from below, careful not to make any sudden noises that might scare Elin away. After a time, they left quietly so the new couple could complete their nest and do what they needed to in peace.

Back at the farmhouse, Terra said, "I'm glad Zeezoo found somebody."

"So am I," said Cyrus. He grabbed a nearly full bottle of one-hundred-proof whiskey from a kitchen cabinet and took it with him to his recliner. He had an intense headache that had lasted nearly all day. His eyes were bloodshot.

"Grandpa, can I ask you something?" said Terra. "Why are there no pictures of people out where you can see them?"

"What do you mean?" asked Cyrus.

"Most of the families I've lived with have pictures of themselves and the people they care about on their walls. And they also put them on tables in nice frames. But you don't have a picture out any-where…not one of anybody."

Cyrus took a sip of whiskey, squinched his eyes, and looked up at his granddaughter. She was now standing beside him, her sweet in-quisitive face looming over his. Terra had no idea that there had once been dozens of old dusty family photographs and portraits on proud display throughout the house, generations of pictures in frames on the walls and in cabinets commemorating the long-ago weddings, births, communions, reunions, graduations, and military services of the Kane family, smiling and brooding photos that marked the gradual and un-broken passage of time.

"I took them all down," said Cyrus. "Years ago."

"What did you do with the pictures?"

Cyrus rose to his feet. "Wait here," he said.

He walked to the end of a dark hallway where all kinds of odds and ends were stored in a closet. When he returned, his arms were filled with several large photo albums and a beat-up shoebox. He took the large stash of photographs to the kitchen and plunked everything onto the table.

"There's more somewhere," said Cyrus. "But this is all I have the energy to find right now."

Terra rushed to pull up a chair at the table next to her grandpa. He pushed aside the albums and brought the shoebox nearer. Then he opened the lid and reached in. The first picture to surface was a faded color snapshot of a smiling middle-aged woman, someone Terra had never seen. The woman had curly red hair that hung past her shoulders in loose ringlets. Dressed in a frilly crop top and denim skirt, she stood in bright sunlight outside the barn, holding two piglets.

"Who's that?" asked Terra.

"Your grandma," said Cyrus. "Grace…that's her name. She was my Gracie." Rubbing his eyes, Cyrus pushed the shoebox in front of Terra. "Here. You can go through all this."

Inside the box were hundreds of photos in no particular order. A few were tied together with rubber bands in little stacks, but most lay separate and loose. Cyrus watched Terra's expressions as she pulled them out one by one. In her young hands, each random frozen moment seemed to defy all his reasoned notions of time and space. The pictures appeared more alive.

Cyrus answered Terra's questions as best he could. He clearly remembered the people and events surrounding certain photos, but with others, he either wasn't around when they were taken or he'd forgotten nearly everything. He stared at one picture of a family picnic and couldn't recall the name of a second cousin on his father's side, or in another, who the tall woman was pitching horseshoes, possibly an acquaintance of his great uncle.

Every picture fascinated Terra, but some more so than others. There were shots of the farm from long ago when it was being worked and thriving. There were several of Terra's mother, Mary, as a little girl, opening presents in front of a Christmas tree, and another of her wearing a fancy yellow dress with a large satin bow at Easter. Terra was especially curious about the people laughing and enjoying a party in an old stack of black-and-white snapshots dated 1956.

About halfway down, Terra came across a creased photo of a young boy sitting on a large tractor. It was her grandpa. Beneath that one was another picture of him as a teenager, bare chested and standing beside a car. Further down, she found a small stack of color snapshots of her grandpa as a handsome young man with green army fatigues, boots, a backpack, and a helmet. He was holding a rifle in some of them.

"Where were these pictures taken, Grandpa?" asked Terra.

"Vietnam," answered Cyrus. It was the first time in many years that he had seen the pictures of his stint in the army, having served in a war he'd never wanted to be a part of.

"Where is that?" asked Terra. "Why did you go there?"

"Vietnam is in Southeast Asia, on the other side of the world. I was drafted into the army and got sent there in 1968."

"What did you do there?"

Cyrus was hesitant because the memories of that time were still painful, even after all these years. In his mind, he weighed how much to tell his granddaughter. Everyone, including Terra, needed to be told the truth about the war in Vietnam, the terrible things that had happened there, the battles, the triumphs and failures, the lives lost, his buddies and thousands of others, but the unvarnished truth could be too brutal for a child to hear. So he was uncertain what to say, torn between leaving out absolutely nothing and telling her just enough to satisfy her curiosity. He chose the latter.

"I was a rifleman in an army platoon that went on reconnaissance patrols through the jungles of Vietnam looking for the enemy," said Cyrus. "They were called the Vietcong."

Terra was mesmerized. "Did you ever find any Vietcong?"

"Yes, I did…many times."

"And what did you do when you found them?"

Again, Cyrus hesitated. His hands were sweating. "I shot at them," he said. "They wanted to kill us. So we had to kill them first. I know it sounds horrible, and it was."

Terra separated the Vietnam photos from the others in the shoebox. "Did you ever kill anyone?" she asked.

"Yes," said Cyrus. He paused to think about how he might explain what he had done. "It was war. They sent me to fight for something I didn't know much about. The Vietcong were killing the people next to me, my friends. I was young and didn't have a choice."

Terra fell silent. The joy of discovering the stash of family photos seemed to have momentarily collapsed into a deep, dark hole. Cyrus could only imagine what she might be thinking.

She picked up each Vietnam photo individually and seemed to be memorizing the visual details. Then she put them aside in a neat stack, all except one, which she separated from the others. She held it in her hand. In the picture, her grandpa was dressed for combat and kneeling next to a Vietnamese boy who looked about her age or slightly younger. Both her grandpa and the boy were facing the camera and smiling. The boy held a little cage with a bird inside.

Terra put the picture on the table between them and pointed to the boy. "Who is this?"

"It's kind of a long story," said Cyrus. He got up and retrieved the whiskey bottle from the other room. He returned, opened it, and took a sip, then sat back down at the table.

"I don't mind," said Terra. "I'd like to hear it."

Cyrus ran his hand through his hair and rubbed his unshaven face. He stared at the photograph. It had been taken so very long ago, but he remembered that day vividly, and the days and weeks just before and after, every detail; they'd never left him.

"A few miles outside our base camp was a small village—not even a village really, just a few scattered shacks and sheds near a rice field," said Cyrus. "Every morning for weeks, we walked through it to get to the jungles where the Vietcong were hiding. Then, every afternoon, we'd walk by the village again on our way back to camp.

"The people in the village were friendly, mostly rice farmers. They owned a few cows, and after a while, we got to know them better. We'd stop and rest there sometimes."

He looked at his granddaughter to see if she was paying attention. She was staring at the photo, listening intently.

"One day—maybe we had gone through the village two dozen times by then—we were tired and stopped to rest. Some of the people came out to greet us. Like I said, they were decent people, friendly for the most part. And this boy, he came up to me holding this little home-made birdcage.

"The boy said, 'A dollar. Buy me. A dollar.' At first I wasn't sure what he was saying or what he wanted. When I got up to leave, he tugged at my shirt and kept smiling at me, pointing at the bird in the cage and repeating, 'A dollar. Buy me. A dollar.' As I was walking away, the boy said, 'He sing pretty for you.'

"That's when I realized, the boy had caught himself a songbird in the wild, and he wanted me to buy it from him for American money, a one-dollar bill."

"Did you buy the bird?" asked Terra.

"Not that day," said Cyrus. "But the next day, when we returned to the village, the boy ran up to me again with the bird, tugging on my uniform and smiling. He followed me everywhere and repeated his offer from the day before. I realized the kid was never going to stop pestering me, so I took a dollar out of my pocket and gave it to him.

"But I didn't understand that he actually wanted me to take the bird. He didn't want charity. A deal was a deal. When he reached inside the cage and grabbed it, I said, 'Wait! No, no! You keep it for me.' I pointed to him and to the bird and said, 'You feed it. You take care of it. You keep the bird for me.'"

Cyrus paused to take a sip of whiskey.

"What happened to the bird?" asked Terra. "Did the boy take care of it for you?"

"Yes. Somehow, even though he only spoke a few fragmented words of English, he understood me. At first, I thought for sure the kid would try selling the songbird to every soldier who passed through the village. But he didn't. He surprised me. When he saw me coming, he'd run to greet me, always with the birdcage in his hands. I'd take a few minutes to sit with him. He sometimes got the bird to sing. He'd say, 'See? Pretty! See?' Anyway, this picture was taken then. I wanted to be able to see his face again when I got back home, if I somehow survived the war."

Cyrus got up and walked over to a window. Along the horizon, the evening sky was darkening. He saw flashes of light and heard faint thunder in the distance.

"It was maybe two weeks later. On our way back from the jungle, we stopped to rest in the village for a few minutes. I was taking a sip of water from my canteen. The boy was sitting beside me, with the bird in its cage. And it began to sing.

"That's when I noticed the barrel of an enemy AK-47 inching out from the shadows in the doorway of one of the shacks. I yelled, 'Sniper!' Someone else shouted, 'Take cover!' It all happened so fast. I grabbed the boy around his waist and ran with him till we were behind some bushes, and I fired back.

"The fight lasted maybe ten minutes. The Vietcong sniper was dead. Two of our men were hit by bullets, but they survived. I checked the boy to make sure he was all right. He was shaking and scared, still holding the cage. We carried the wounded men back to our camp. An incident report was filed. Our lieutenant had to explain to our commanders what happened, where, and how."

The rumble outside and flashes of lightning were closer now. Cyrus turned to look at his granddaughter. She was staring back at him, wide-eyed.

"Did you see the boy after that?" asked Terra.

"At dawn the next morning, two of our jets flew over the village and dropped napalm on everyone there. It didn't matter if the people were innocent, or guilty in some way—old men and women, children, babies. The whole place, everything, exploded in fireballs and was burned to the ground in less than an hour."

Cyrus rubbed his eyes. Over the years, he had refused to talk about his time in the war. He'd never told his story to anyone, not even his wife when she was alive.

"I volunteered to go with a group of men back to the village to see if there were any survivors. When we arrived, the shacks were still smoldering. I found the boy lying face up near the footpath. His eyes were open, so I closed them. The little cage was on the ground beside him, the bird inside, unhurt. I reached in, took it out, and held it. I wanted to feel its feathers, soft and fluttering. I could feel its heartbeat.

"And I let it go."

Terra stood up and came over to her grandpa. She put her arms around him.

"The boy's name was Xuan," said Cyrus. "But I could never say it quite right. So I made up a nickname for him. I called him Zeezoo."

The rains came and lasted well into the night.

10

Working as a team, Zeezoo and Elin finished the nest. The next morning, Elin laid her first egg. She laid one egg a day until five grayish speckled eggs were nestled beneath her to warm and look after. Zeezoo proudly kept watch outside the hole. Every few hours, he relieved Elin, taking his turn to sit on the eggs for a short while so she could stretch her wings and find something to eat.

Although Elin missed her sisters, she thought the woodland just beyond the farm was a fine place to raise a family of her own. Zeezoo loved her deeply, and now that they were together, he couldn't imagine life without Elin by his side. Day and night, he protected and watched over her and their clutch of eggs.

Zeezoo's new responsibilities prevented him from spending much time at the farmhouse. On the weekends and after school, Terra visited the nest, careful not to talk loudly or cause a fuss. He was always happy to see her and greeted her each time with a kiss on the cheek. Over time, Elin began to understand that Cyrus and Terra were an important part of Zeezoo's life and not a threat to her or the eggs.

Ever vigilant for predators and other trouble, Zeezoo settled into a routine in and around the nest. He flew high over the canopy of trees, scanning the area. At night, he listened carefully for the telltale rustling sounds of creatures stealthily stalking their prey on the ground below. He ate when he could and barely slept.

Then something happened. It was past nightfall a week after the fifth egg was laid. Elin had fallen asleep on the nest. Perched nearby on a large limb, Zeezoo was resting his eyes and beginning to nod off when he heard a faint sound. Somewhere in the darkness, someone was moving steadily through the underbrush.

The rustling of brush was a fair distance away but fast approaching. Zeezoo decided to investigate before whatever was lurking in the woods came any closer to the nest. He checked on Elin and quickly flew by moonlight through the trees toward the sound.

A dozen yards or so from the ominous rustle of leaves being softly brushed aside and twigs snapping, Zeezoo landed silently on an overhead branch and hid in the shadows. He waited for the intruder to pass beneath him.

As the figure stepped across a small open area between two trees, the moon and starlight shone fleetingly upon the intruder's face. It was Edgar.

Certain that Edgar posed a serious danger to Elin and their eggs, Zeezoo tried to think of a way to prevent the prowling cat from coming any closer to the nest. He followed Edgar for a minute or two, flitting from tree to tree, to see if the cat might veer off in a different direction, but he didn't. Something had to be done.

From his perch, Zeezoo dove and landed on Edgar's back, high up near the cat's neck. Edgar shrieked and bucked like a rodeo bull. He jumped and spun around violently. Zeezoo hung on.

"Get off me!" shouted Edgar, unable to see whom or what had attacked him.

Zeezoo dug his feet and long claws into Edgar's skin before leaping off and flying to a low nearby limb just beyond the cat's reach. Edgar sprang angrily to try to grab Zeezoo but fell hard on his nose, empty-handed.

"Zeezoo! I'm gonna kill you!" yelled Edgar.

"I don't think so," said Zeezoo. "Tell me, Edgar. What are you doing out here in the woods?"

Edgar jumped as high as he could, trying to snag Zeezoo, but again he fell short. Zeezoo was just out of reach above his head. "I came looking for you," said Edgar. "I heard you were back and brought a friend. Did you think I wouldn't find out about your nest?"

"That's what I thought," said Zeezoo.

"It's just a matter of time," snarled Edgar. "I'm going to find your nest. And when I do, nothing will stop me from destroying everything you care about."

"Tell me why!" demanded Zeezoo. "What have I ever done to you?"

Edgar sat upright on his haunches, his tail swishing back and forth. "It's nothing personal," he answered calmly. "I enjoy catching birds and ending them."

"It's not right," said Zeezoo.

"No! You're wrong," growled Edgar. "Catching and eating birds and other living things is natural for a cat like me. I was born to kill. It's in me to kill you."

"But you know me," said Zeezoo.

"And you think that matters," said Edgar.

"Maybe it should."

Edgar licked his paw, got up, and paced in a circle beneath Zeezoo. "At the farmhouse, I have to be careful. If anyone ever found your bones and feathers, they'd suspect me. You're protected there because they look after you, but out here, they'll never know what happened."

From the safety of his perch, Zeezoo looked into Edgar's eyes and saw not a trace of compassion in them. He knew what Edgar had said was true. A cat's nature was true for a cat. A sparrow's nature and spirit were unique and different. And nature, Zeezoo knew, could be both a wonderful and terrible thing.

"I'll find where your nest is," repeated Edgar.

"Be careful where you step," said Zeezoo.

"What do you mean?"

"I have a friend, and he's laid traps for you all over these woods." The bluff came to Zeezoo's mind in a flash. He disliked lying, but what choice did he have? It was the only threat he thought Edgar might believe.

"What kind of traps?" asked Edgar.

"He's made several types," said Zeezoo. "There are deep camouflaged holes with razor-sharp spikes in the bottom of them, dug for you to fall into. And snares to snatch your legs and dangle you under a tree for his dinner."

"You're lying."

"Am I?" said Zeezoo. "Tell me, Edgar. Why are there no other cats wandering around out here in the woods except you? Why is that?"

"What are you saying?"

"It's obvious, isn't it? He's eaten them all."

"What is this thing that eats cats?" Edgar fidgeted. His head turned this way and that, and his eyes thought they saw things that weren't there.

"Everyone in the woods is afraid of him. He's a cat skinner, but because he and I are good friends, I call him 'Skinner,' and he calls me 'Z.Z.,'" answered Zeezoo. "Lucky for me, he doesn't like the taste of birds. I got caught in one of his snares once, but he let me go if I promised to help him catch a few cats."

"How do I know you're not lying to save your own skin?" Edgar responded.

"Do you feel that?" asked Zeezoo. "Do you feel the hair on your back standing on end? That's how you can tell the skinner is nearby, getting ready to pounce. Here's the truth, Edgar. I've been stalling this whole time so he can get close enough to catch you."

The hair on Edgar's back was indeed rising. Behind him he heard a slight rustle of leaves giving way to a nighttime breeze. Quickly, he turned around to see if it was the dreaded cat skinner. Zeezoo didn't hesitate. He leapt from his perch, aiming his beak straight at Edgar's backside.

Edgar screamed and began to run, never looking back. Zeezoo continued his aerial attack, jabbing and nipping at Edgar's rear end all the way out of the woods. Once they were in the field, Zeezoo broke off the assault and hid in some tall weeds. He watched the frightened cat race across the field to the farmhouse.

Confident Edgar wouldn't return, Zeezoo rushed back to the nest. Elin was awake. "Where did you go?" she asked.

"I thought I heard something."

"What was it?"

"Nothing," said Zeezoo.

11

The bag of sweet corn seed lay half hidden behind a wheelbarrow and stack of old dirty rakes and hoes in a corner of the barn. Terra spotted it early one morning while helping her grandpa feed and brush Lizzie.

After combing Lizzie's mane and gathering three eggs from the hens, Terra rushed to check out the bag. She moved the gardening tools aside and opened the large sack. Inside there was still seed. After reaching in, she scooped a handful and poured them into her jeans pocket.

Terra approached Cyrus, who was moving about in the goat pen with a metal bucket, filling their trough with clean water. She held out several of the seeds she had discovered for him to see. "Grandpa, look what I found," she said excitedly. "Can we grow some corn?"

Cyrus stopped what he was doing and inspected the seeds. "Where did you get these?"

"In the barn. There's a big bag of it."

It took a moment, but her grandpa remembered the leftover bag of corn seed. "I'm sorry," said Cyrus. "Those seeds are at least eight to ten years old. I should've thrown them away. After a couple of years, they go bad and won't germinate. You have to plant the seeds soon after you buy them."

Terra reached into her pocket and took out the seeds. "So you're saying they're dead?"

"Yes, dear," said Cyrus. He finished with the goats, whose names now were "Thor" and "Loki." Terra had decided to name them after two popular comic book characters who were also brothers. "Listen, your bus will be here in about thirty minutes. You need to get your backpack and school stuff ready. I made your lunch. It's in the refrigerator."

Disappointed, Terra returned to the barn with her handful of seeds, ready to toss them back into the bag with the others. But then she thought, *If they're already dead, why can't I just bury them in the ground? I could make a wish and see what happens.*

Written on the front of the corn seed bag were the following instructions: "Plant seeds 1 to 2 inches deep and 6 to 10 inches apart. Rows should be spaced 30 to 36 inches apart. Water well at planting time."

Terra had just enough seeds in her hand to plant a row. She ran to the edge of the old garden bed near the house and got down on her hands and knees. After pulling out several scraggly weeds and combing the dirt with her fingers to make it looser, she planted a short row of corn seeds. She then went into the farmhouse to fetch water in a pitcher and poured it over them.

Cyrus watched her from the chicken coop. "It's time! The bus will be here. Hurry!" he shouted.

Terra went back into the house to get her school stuff and walked quickly with her grandpa to the main road. The bus was a few minutes late.

During morning recess, outside near the basketball courts, Terra met up with her three new best friends and classmates: Nikki, Desiree, and Cleo.

"You're so lucky to have your own bedroom, Terra," said Cleo. "I have to share a room with my little sister. It's the worst! She gets into all my stuff."

Both Nikki and Desiree chimed in. "Oh, my God! I know!"

"It must be really great having a closet all to yourself, Terra," said Nikki. She wrinkled her nose. "My mom makes me wear my two older sister's hand-me-down clothes, even though they sweated like pigs in them and everything!"

"Ewww!" echoed the other girls.

"Tell us more about Zeezoo," said Desiree. "Will he fly to anyone who calls him, or does he just come to you?"

"He'll come to my grandpa," answered Terra. "I'm not sure about other people, but if he saw you were nice and weren't going to hurt him, he probably would. I think I'd have to be with you the first time you tried."

"How much longer will it be until you get to see the baby sparrows?" asked Cleo.

"Grandpa says he thinks they'll hatch sometime next week," said Terra. "I can't wait to see them."

"How many eggs are there?" asked Nikki.

"I'm not allowed to climb the tree to look because it might scare away the mama bird. So we don't know how many babies are in the nest. After they're born, maybe you guys could come over to my house and see them. Maybe you can even spend the night. I could ask my grandpa."

"Sounds good to me," said Desiree. "I'd like to come over and see your place."

"If your grandpa says you can have a sleepover, I'll talk to my mom to see if she'll let me come," said Nikki.

"I'll ask my mom too," said Cleo.

Just then, two boys who were determined to scare the other kids during recess ran up to the girls' pleasant gathering, bared their teeth, and roared like lions. Three of the girls reacted as expected, running away and squealing loudly, the boys giving chase. Only Terra stood her ground.

On the far corner of one basketball court, a group of kids were playing four square. Closer to the edge of the schoolyard, others stood in line waiting for their turn to play tetherball. A dozen or so more in the grass field were joined in a friendly game of red rover, shouting back and forth about whom to "send over."

Most days, Terra participated in the games, but today she just wanted to watch. She walked over to the red rover game and cheered for the side that was losing. Terra liked red rover because at the end of the game, everyone winds up being on the winning team.

The first matchup ended, and fresh sides were being chosen for a second game when an older boy came up from behind and tapped Terra on the shoulder. "There's someone who wants to talk to you," he said.

"Who?" asked Terra.

"I don't know. It's some lady. She's over there by the fence."

Terra turned around to see who it might be. Across the schoolyard, standing on the far side of a chain link fence that separated school property from the street, stood a familiar figure.

"Mom!" shouted Terra.

Terra ran to her. Crying, she rushed out a gate onto the sidewalk, and they embraced. Her mother, Mary, kissed her face. "I've missed you, Mom!" Terra sobbed, tears flowing down her cheeks.

"My baby girl! I've missed you too." Mary took out a clean tissue from her oversize handbag and wiped Terra's wet eyes. "There, there. Please don't cry."

At first, amid their frantic hugs and kisses, neither could say anything to the other except "I love you, Terra" and "I love you, Mom."

After a minute or two, Terra stepped back to look her mother over. She appeared thinner and much older, especially in the face, than Terra remembered. Her mom's eyes had dark rings under them, like she hadn't slept in a while. She didn't smell at all clean, and her clothes, jeans and a light-blue chambray shirt, were badly soiled and tattered.

"Are you okay, Mom?" asked Terra. She gazed into her mother's eyes.

"Listen, Terra. We're getting out of here. You need to come with me." Her mom's voice sounded a little slurred. She took Terra firmly by the hand and began to walk.

"But why, Mom?" Terra was confused. "Where are we going?"

"Somewhere far from here, baby." Her mom's eyes darted from side to side as if some danger lurked close by. Her expression was one of concern and no longer warm.

Terra stopped. "I don't understand. Why do we have to go?"

"I'll explain later," answered Mary.

The school bell rang, marking the end of morning recess. From somewhere near the basketball courts, her friend Desiree shouted, "Terra, come on!" Terra saw her classmates walking to the main building and lining up at the door. Reluctantly, she let go of her mother's hand.

"Mom, I need to go back," said Terra. "I like my teacher and school, and I don't want to get in trouble. If you go to the front desk in the office, you can sign me out there. They'll come get me, okay?"

Mary grabbed her daughter by the wrist and yanked her close. "Please, baby. I don't have time for this. We have to leave right now!"

Except for a few stray clouds that looked like fluffy white islands floating along on a silent sea, the sky was a brilliant blue. Terra followed her mother block after block, down streets lined with nice homes, surrounded by manicured green lawns. Busier roads butted up against rows of businesses of various kinds. The two spoke little as they walked.

Eventually they came to a multistoried apartment building in an older part of downtown. A large yellow tabby cat lay asleep on a concrete step near the front door. Leaning her head out an upstairs window, a woman with a wide chubby face was shouting down at an elderly man stepping out of a car. He didn't look up or respond. Instead, he got back in his car and drove off.

Mary and her daughter went inside and took an elevator to the fifth floor. At the end of a dimly lit hallway, Mary knocked at a door. A man with black bushy hair, a thick goatee, and dark eyes opened it. He wore a white tank top, and his arms were covered in tattoos.

The man glared at Mary. "Do you have my money?" he asked sternly.

"I've got it," answered Mary, "but I need more."

The man moved aside and ushered them in. Terra stood next to her mother and looked around. The small apartment had lots of leafy green plants lined up near the window and a playpen filled with infant toys in the corner. Behind a closed bedroom door next to her, Terra heard two women's muffled voices talking in a foreign language and a baby fussing.

"Who is this with you?" asked the man. He walked over to the sofa, sat, and grabbed a pack of cigarettes off the coffee table.

"This is my daughter," said Mary.

"Interesting," said the man. "I didn't know you had a daughter. You've never mentioned her. Does she have a name?"

"My name is Terra. What's yours?"

Terra's mother grabbed her arm and squeezed it. The unspoken message was clear: to shut her mouth and not say another word.

"I'm Stanislav, little girl," answered the man. He retrieved a lighter from his pants pocket, lit a cigarette, and took a long puff. He blew a large ring of smoke that gently floated straight toward Terra's face. She brushed aside the foul-smelling smoke with a wave of her hand before it had a chance to get on her.

"So where's my money?" asked Stanislav.

Mary reached deep into her large handbag, and after a bit of digging, she pulled out a fat roll of green bills. She walked over to the coffee table and threw it down. Stanislav smiled, leaned forward, and peeled the bills apart, counting how much was there, then rolled them back together. He flung the money back onto the table.

"Is this a joke?" said Stanislav loudly. "There's only two thousand here. Where's the rest of it?" He rose and came close to Mary until his nose was just inches from hers.

"This is all I owe you," said Mary, her voice tense.

Stanislav took a step back and laughed. "You understand how things work. I know you do. My boss isn't going to accept this." He said it in a relaxed, methodic way. "And you shouldn't have brought your daughter here."

He paused to take a long puff of his cigarette. "When you don't pay back what you owe in a timely manner, Mary, you have to expect difficult consequences. And there's also the fact you owe a good deal of interest. You're short at least three thousand dollars."

"I'm trying. Please believe me," said Mary. "Please. I just need a little more time to come up with it."

"That's the trouble: I don't trust you," growled Stanislav. "You have a long history of lying. The truth doesn't mean anything to an addict like you. All you care about is how to kill the pain you feel inside. That's why you keep coming around here, to get more and more of my special pills. You can't live without them." He took another drag of his cigarette. "Tell me, when is the last time you popped a pill to ease the suffering? It was just before you came here this morning, wasn't it? I can see it in your eyes. You're buzzed right now."

"Leave my mom alone!" said Terra. "You got your money, mister. She's not giving you another dime." She tugged on her mother's arm to leave. "Let's go, Mom."

Mary didn't move.

Stanislav glared at Terra but said nothing. He went into the room where the women had been talking and a baby had been fussing and returned with a plastic baggie filled with blue pills.

He handed the baggie to Mary and smiled at Terra. "This, my dear child, is why your poor mother will do whatever I say, and pay me whatever amount I want."

Mary stuffed the baggie into her handbag. "I'll pay you back," she said. "I promise. It'll take a couple of days."

"I have no doubt you will," said Stanislav. "Because if you don't come up with the money you owe us—and I mean all of it and very soon—we'll come looking for you…and your daughter."

He turned to Terra. "Let me give you a bit of advice, little one." He looked her in the eyes. "If you'd prefer not to end up like your druggie mother, don't ever go into debt. And if you do borrow from others, make sure you repay them quickly. Debt can be a powerful tool. It can be your key to nice things and a better life. But if not handled wisely, it also can mean loss of freedom and death."

Terra didn't cower from Stanislav's menacing gaze. Instead, she kept her eyes fixed on his. "Can we go now, Mom?" she asked.

"Yes," answered Mary. "We're done here."

"But first can I have something cold to drink?" Terra directed her question directly to Stanislav. She crossed her arms around her stomach and groaned. "We walked a long way, and I'm thirsty. I don't feel too good."

"I'll see what we have," answered Stanislav.

He disappeared into a small kitchen just off the main room. Terra heard him first searching in a cupboard, then moving jars and other things in a refrigerator. "There's water, tea, and soda," said Stanislav. "Which do you want?"

Terra doubled over and grimaced. "Mom, I got a bad cramp. I feel like I might throw up. Can you see what kind of soda he has and bring one to me?"

"Sure, baby." Mary rushed to help Stanislav and returned a minute later, carrying a glass filled with root beer and ice. "Do you need to lie down somewhere for a while?"

With Stanislav looking on, Terra took the drink from her mother and slugged it down in one gulp. She handed the glass to Stanislav and stumbled backward slightly. "Thank you," she said. "I'm starting to feel a little better."

"Are you sure?" asked Mary. "When did you start to feel like this?" She placed the back of her hand against Terra's forehead and neck to feel if she had a fever.

"It came over me all of a sudden," said Terra. "Maybe I just needed something to drink."

The two turned to leave. Terra opened the door. "It was nice meeting you, mister. Thank you for the root beer. Now let's get out of here, Mom."

When they were halfway out the door, Stanislav grabbed Mary by the arm and spun her around. "Don't forget what I said," he snarled, bringing his face once again closer to hers. "I expect to see you soon with the rest of the money." With a hard shove, he let go of her.

On their way back to the elevator, Terra took her mother's hand and ran. "Hurry, Mom," she whispered.

The elevator appeared to be stuck on a different floor above them. After pushing the button several times, Terra said, "Come on! Let's take the stairs." She led her mother to an emergency stairwell at the other end of the hallway.

Once they were outside the apartment building, she didn't stop pulling her mother along quickly until they were three or four blocks away. "Slow down, Terra! Wait!" said Mary, out of breath. "Why are you rushing me? I need to rest for a minute."

Nearby, a homeless man with a long gray beard slept under an awning in front of an empty storefront. His head lay on a leather guitar case. Several large pigeons were cooing and inspecting his belongings. Two well-dressed women holding several shopping bags walked out of a clothing boutique then disappeared into a shoe outlet next door. Three men in suits, one of them talking on his cell phone, were waiting for the red light to change at a crosswalk.

"Do you have your own place, Mom?" asked Terra. "Somewhere we can go?"

Mary hung her head. "No. I was going to buy us two bus tickets, so we could make a new start together somewhere far from here. But the money I had is gone. I stupidly gave it all to Stanislav. I don't know what I was thinking." She paused for a moment and sighed. "Ever since your father died, I've wanted to feel numb. I'm not a strong-willed person, Terra. I'm weak. Please forgive me."

"What do we do now?" asked Terra.

"You must be getting hungry. We both need to find something to eat. But without any money, I'm not sure where we can go."

"Maybe this will help." Terra reached into her pants pocket and pulled out a large wad of bills. It was the two thousand dollars her mother had given Stanislav.

"Oh my God!" said Mary. "Put it back in your pocket before anyone sees it. Oh my God. He's going to come looking for us. What have you done?"

12

In the restroom at the Greyhound bus station, Terra watched her mother swallow one of the blue pills from the baggie. Mary fixed her face in a mirror and hid the rest of the pills in her handbag under the roll of cash and two bus tickets. It would be another half hour before boarding began.

Terra sat next to her mother on a bench. The bus station's indoor waiting area was crowded. Most of the people around them appeared to be traveling alone. Some were busy messing with their cell phones. A suitcase or backpack lay by their feet. There were families with kids, but not many, as well as several couples sitting together. One clean-cut middle-aged man kept digging through papers in a briefcase. A lady with dark eyeliner and tattoos paced the room and spoke to herself. Every so often, she thrust her fist in the air.

"Mom, I want to stay with Grandpa," blurted Terra, unable to hold it in any longer. She loved her mother with all her heart, but everything was happening too fast. "He's been good to me. I like it there. Why can't we all live together on the farm?"

"Don't make this difficult," said Mary. "You're with me now, and we're not going back there, not ever."

Terra noticed her mother's arms and legs were shaking and her skin looked sweaty. "But what about Grandpa? He's going to wonder where I am."

"Forget him. You don't know your grandfather like I do," said Mary.

"But why, Mom? Why are you mad? What did Grandpa do?"

"You're better off not knowing."

"Tell me!" said Terra. "Grandpa's a good person. He'd never hurt anyone on purpose."

A man's voice came over a loudspeaker announcing it would soon be time for passengers to show their tickets and begin boarding the bus. He urged everyone to gather their belongings and form a line near the bus. A collective murmur emanated throughout the waiting area as people stood and got out their tickets.

Mary went to get up but stumbled and almost fell. Terra grabbed her mother firmly by the arm to steady her. "Are you okay?" she asked.

"I feel fine," answered Mary, as she tried again to stand. She straightened herself, took three or four steps forward, then stopped. "Where are we?" she asked.

"We're at the bus station," answered Terra, confused. "Is something wrong?"

Without warning, Mary's eyes closed, and her body collapsed, toppling backward onto the tile floor.

Terra dropped to her knees next to her but didn't know what to do. She patted her mother's face. "Mom!" she yelled. "Somebody, please help my mom!"

A half dozen people came quickly and hovered over Terra and her mother. One man dropped to the floor and felt Mary's wrist and neck. "I don't feel a pulse," he said. "Hurry. Somebody call 911!"

"What's wrong with my mom?" cried Terra.

"I'm not sure, but we're going to help her," said the man. "Do you know if she took anything? Is she on any kind of medication?"

"She took a pill. It was blue…a little while ago."

From behind the ticket and information counter, one of the Greyhound staff, a tall man, came running. He asked Terra to step back while he and the other man checked her mother's vital signs. "Hang in there, lady," he said loudly. "Did anyone call 911?"

For Terra, time seemed to stand still. A minute felt like an eternity. Everything around her seemed to move in slow motion as more people who were simply curious to see what the commotion was about crowded near her mother and jostled for a better view.

The sound of a police siren approached and a patrol car's blue-and-red flashing lights spilled through the windows into the room. A uniformed officer rushed in with a large EMS satchel slung over his shoulder and knelt beside Mary. "Does anyone know what happened?" he asked.

"This girl says her mother took some kind of blue pill," said the first man to come to Mary's aid, now standing beside the officer.

The officer checked Mary's pulse and pupils. "It was probably OxyContin. She's dying from an opioid overdose," said the officer. "How long has she been unconscious?"

"It's been a few minutes," one of the onlookers said.

The officer motioned to the Greyhound employee. "Get over on the other side of her body and gently lean her head back." The employee did as told. The officer reached into his satchel and brought out a small white package that read "Narcan." He peeled away the wrapping, placed the nozzle of the spray device a short way up Mary's nose, and pushed in the plunger. After administering a burst of overdose reversal medicine, he rolled Mary onto her side and looked at his watch.

"Come on, lady," said the officer. "Come on. Wake up!"

Terra watched in horror. Her mother lay on the floor as if sleeping, limp. She wanted to scream, but what good would it do? She felt like crying, but no tears flowed. An older woman behind Terra grabbed her by the shoulders and held onto her. "Don't worry," said the woman. "It'll be okay."

The officer continued to talk to Mary, urging her to wake up, but after two minutes, she remained lifeless and unresponsive. Swiftly, he rolled Mary onto her back, opened another Narcan, and gave her a second dose. "Come on!" he barked. "I'm not going to let you die on me! Wake up!"

After another two minutes, he leaned back and looked up. Everything went still. An unworldly quiet filled the room. Then everyone heard a gasp. Mary opened her eyes and sat upright. Her expression was as if nothing had happened.

Cyrus glanced at the clock on the wall. The time for Terra's bus to have returned with her from school had come and gone. He sluggishly rose from the recliner and stretched. Next to his feet, a half-filled bottle of whiskey lay on its side. He bent over, picked up the bottle, and took it to the kitchen.

"Terra," he called out. "Are you here?" When she didn't answer, he stepped outside and looked around. There was no trace of her. He thought for a moment. "Maybe she's with Zeezoo."

He walked across the field, overgrown with wild flowers and weeds, toward where the sparrows' nest lay hidden in the woods. At its edge, he hollered for his granddaughter, "Terra! Can you hear me? Terra! Where are you?"

Watching out for predators from a high limb near the nest, Zeezoo heard Cyrus calling for Terra. "I'll be back soon," he told Elin. In a flash, he leapt into the air and flew off to see his friend.

Zeezoo landed on Cyrus' shoulder.

"Have you seen Terra?" asked Cyrus.

Zeezoo chirped once for "no."

"I don't think she came home on the bus," said Cyrus. He was starting to become concerned. He looked back toward the barn and chicken coop. "But maybe she's around somewhere playing. Can you help me look for her?"

Two chirps, and Zeezoo sped off in the direction of the barn. While Cyrus searched the chicken coop, pens, barn, smokehouse, and storage sheds, Zeezoo scanned the entire farm from above. He searched the far corners of the field, the creek, and both sides of the highway where Terra always got on and off the school bus.

Zeezoo returned and rested atop a fencepost near the barn. "Any sign of her?" asked Cyrus.

The sparrow chirped once.

"I'd better check at the school," said Cyrus. Since he still didn't own a working house phone or cell phone, he had no choice but to drive there.

"Do you want to come along?" Zeezoo chirped twice. Cyrus got in his pickup truck and rolled down the windows. "Get in."

Twenty minutes later, Cyrus pulled into the school parking lot. Two police cruisers were near the front door with their lights flashing, along with a third car he recognized. It belonged to Roberta Johnson.

She came out of the building and met him. The look on her face was one of serious concern. "I'm very glad to see you, Mr. Kane, but you need to promise me that before this week is out, you're going to buy yourself a cell phone. You can't go on living in the past like you do. You have to stop shutting yourself off from the rest of the world. I need a faster, better way to get in touch with you."

Cyrus nodded. "Where is Terra?"

"She's not here," Roberta answered. "According to some of the children, she was seen leaving the school grounds on foot with a woman. Based on their description of her, we think it might have been Mary, but we're not sure."

"Did anyone see which direction they went?"

"That way, toward town, we think. The police already have searched the immediate area around the school, but there's no sign of the two."

A police officer got out of his car and walked up to them. "I've checked with dispatch to see if there might be some leads we can go on," he said. "They say there was an incident at the bus station. The report says a woman overdosed on opioids, and she had a young girl with her. Neither of them would give their name."

"Where are they now?" asked Roberta.

"The woman was revived and taken by ambulance to the hospital for blood tests and observation. They told me an officer drove the girl to the hospital separately. That's all they have in the report."

Cyrus jumped into his truck.

Roberta chased after him. "What are you doing, Mr. Kane?" she asked as he began to pull away.

"I'm going to the hospital."

A few minutes later, Cyrus pulled up outside the hospital's emergency entrance and rushed in. At the reception desk, a nurse intervened and tried to answer his questions. "We were supposed to receive an overdose patient earlier," she said, "but she was never checked in. When the paramedics arrived and opened the ambulance doors, she ran off.

"An officer later brought a young girl into the waiting room, but after we told them the woman had run away, the girl became upset. He tried to calm her down, but when his back was turned, she vanished. That was a few hours ago." The nurse then described to Cyrus what the girl looked like.

Cyrus hurried back to his truck and got in. He sat quietly behind the wheel and tried to think of where his granddaughter might have gone. After a minute or so, he turned to Zeezoo. "I'm sure Terra was here. She couldn't have gotten too far. Listen, I have an idea. We can cover more ground and find her faster if we split up. I'll drive around and search the streets in this area. I want you to fly overhead and see if you can spot her. I'll meet you back here in a half hour. Okay?"

Zeezoo chirped twice and flew off.

From the roof of a nearby building, Zeezoo searched for Terra, but the surrounding structures and budding spring leaves on the trees obscured the world below. He leapt from his perch and flew straight up in the air to get a better view, but the higher he went, the harder it was to tell anyone apart on the ground. The people all looked like insects. He had no choice but to come back down and hunt for her much closer to the street.

For Zeezoo, who wasn't accustomed to the orderly turmoil of urban traffic, flying closer to earth proved dangerous. He narrowly dodged a fast-moving vehicle and was almost hit by another as he raced down one street, up another, and across a number of busy intersections, combing the area for his young friend. Several times, he spotted children walking or playing with other kids, but none of them were Terra.

Unable to find her anywhere, Zeezoo landed atop a lamppost. He needed to rest his wings and catch his breath. It was time to return to the hospital parking lot and meet up with Cyrus. He fluffed his feathers and glanced around one last time.

That's when he spotted Terra. Immediately, he recognized her silhouette. She was across the road, sitting on a wooden bench along a bicycle path, alone.

Quickly, Zeezoo flew to her. He landed on Terra's lap, looked up at her, and chirped noisily several times. She was staring into space, detached from everything. Her eyes were red and swollen from crying. At first, she didn't respond or even acknowledge his presence.

"She left me..." Terra's words materialized, faint and colorless. She wiped her eyes with her shirtsleeve. "Everyone leaves," she sniffled. "My dad, my friends, my mom. They don't stay." She reached out her hand and gently stroked Zeezoo's head, felt his soft feathers. He kept very still and let her pet him. "But you stay, don't you Zeezoo?" Terra looked down and gazed at him. A brief smile appeared. "You and Grandpa."

There were other people on the bicycle path, several joggers out for a late-afternoon run, an older couple on matching bicycles, two gossiping women in lockstep with each other, and a young mother pushing a stroller. Her baby was sleeping.

Zeezoo simply being near Terra seemed to calm her. "How did you find me?" she asked. He hopped onto her shoulder and tugged her hair firmly with his beak. It was time to get back.

"If you're here, then maybe Grandpa is close by too," said Terra. "Did he come with you?"

Zeezoo chirped twice, tugged again at Terra's hair, and flew off toward the sidewalk along the street. He came back to her and repeated this three or four times. Eventually she understood what Zeezoo was trying to communicate. She got up and followed him.

A short time later, they reached the hospital parking lot where Cyrus stood waiting next to his pickup truck for Zeezoo's return. Beside him was Roberta Johnson. When the two saw Terra, they raced to her. Terra cried a little, but the tears were fleeting.

Zeezoo watched and listened. He understood that no one wanted to talk too much about what had happened. Mostly, they were glad Terra was safe and with people who cared about her. There were many questions but few answers.

"I'm really, really hungry, Grandpa," said Terra. "Can we please get something to eat?"

"Sure, we can," answered Cyrus. He promised to follow up with Roberta later.

The next day, Cyrus drove to Children and Family Services and gave Roberta what little additional information his granddaughter had divulged to him so she could file a report. Afterward, he went to a store and bought two smartphones, one for himself and the other for Terra.

13

After ten days of patiently sitting on her eggs, Elin felt her unborn babies stir beneath her. From inside each of the shells, she heard their weak little voices talking to her. They wanted to tell her how much they loved and appreciated her and how anxious they were to break free of their snug confines and see the world.

The following morning, Elin called for Zeezoo. He arrived quickly. "What is it?" he asked.

"It's happening," answered Elin.

Huddled together, they stood on the edge of the nest and watched. There was a cracking, and soon the first hatchling poked its bald gray-and-pink head out from its shell. Within a few hours, there were five new faces in the nest. Their eyes were closed, but when they heard their parents joyously greeting them, their mouths opened in unison; they were already hungry.

Before long, a chorus of youthful chirping echoed from the tall pine. Zeezoo and Elin busied themselves with feeding the babies. They took turns catching insects, caterpillars, grubs, and worms for their newborns to eat. Although there was a lot of pushing and shoving among the three brothers and two sisters in the nest, Zeezoo and Elin made sure each child got their fair share of food.

Like she did nearly every day after school, Terra came to the nest to check on things. When she heard the chicks, she exclaimed, "Yay!" And then she turned and ran back across the field to the farmhouse, yelling, "They're here, Grandpa! The babies are here!"

A short while later, Terra returned with her grandpa. Cyrus made his way through the brush, looked up, and listened. "I'm happy for them," he said. "It sounds like they've got a full nest."

"Can I see them?" Terra asked excitedly.

"No," said Cyrus. "I don't want you climbing the tree, maybe hurting yourself and disrupting the nest."

She grabbed her grandpa's arm and begged, "Please! Please let me see them!"

Finally he relented. "It's up to Zeezoo," he said.

Zeezoo and Elin were so busy chasing down bugs and feeding them to their newborn chicks that neither of them noticed Cyrus and Terra at first. The two new parents flew swiftly through the woods and back to the nest, always returning with a squirming beetle, cricket, or something else alive in their beaks.

With her grandpa beside her, Terra quietly observed the two sparrows' movements. She thought, *They look like a poem. Maybe love is like this, a feathered thing flying past and not attached to some blank page in a book.*

Cyrus whistled for Zeezoo.

In seconds, he swooped down and greeted them affectionately. Cyrus congratulated Zeezoo and asked him if it was all right if Terra looked in on the babies. Zeezoo cocked his head and flew to Elin. Less than a minute later, he returned. Two chirps.

Cyrus lifted his granddaughter to a sturdy branch. From there, Terra carefully climbed several limbs until she reached the old woodpecker hole. With Elin and Zeezoo looking on, she peered inside.

"One, two, three…four…" counted Terra. "Grandpa, there are five!"

"That's wonderful," said Cyrus.

The newborn chicks heard Terra. Instinctively, they stretched out their necks, opened their beaks for food as if she were their mother, and chirped. To Terra, their five wide-open mouths pointing straight up, all open at the same time, looked hilarious, and she laughed.

"Be careful not to touch them," said her grandpa. "Mama birds don't like it if you do."

"I won't," she answered. "I promise."

Terra remembered that she had her brand-new cell phone in her pants pocket. Holding tightly onto a branch with one hand, she carefully took it out with the other, pushed the camera icon, and snapped a picture of the chicks to send to her friends. Then she held her phone out and took a selfie, smiling with the new babies.

"What are you doing?" asked Cyrus.

Terra went to answer him, but in the very next breath, her phone slipped out of her hand. For a moment, it popped up in the air like a wet bar of soap. She tried to grab it but missed and lost her balance. Both feet slipped off the branch. She screamed and toppled, arms flailing as she crashed face-first through the pine branches. She landed, not with a thud, but softly in her grandpa's arms. He'd been standing directly beneath her the whole while, just in case.

"Are you all right?" he asked.

She had some minor cuts and scrapes on her arms but otherwise looked fine. "I think so," Terra said, her voice a little shaky. "Thank you for catching me."

Cyrus set his granddaughter down and looked for her phone; he found it lying nearby. An abundant layer of dead pine needles on the ground had cushioned its fall, and the phone didn't have a scratch on it.

He handed the phone back to Terra. "See? This is my problem with new technology," he said. "If you're not careful, it will get you killed. Promise me you'll be more careful in the future."

"I will, Grandpa."

Neither Zeezoo nor Elin seemed fazed by Terra's near catastrophe. The five newborn chicks were chirping. Both parents had resumed their duties, swiftly flying off in search of more insects and returning moments later with something to eat.

Cyrus nudged Terra. "We should leave now so they can care for their chicks without us getting in the way and distracting them. You and I can come back later to look in on their progress."

"Okay," said Terra. She smiled at her grandpa.

Since landing back on the ground, Terra had already texted her friends from school and sent everyone pics of the baby sparrows, including her hard-won selfie. Before she and her grandpa even made it to the field, Terra received three replies: "How cute!" "Congrats!" and a smiley face.

14

The next morning, Zeezoo was returning to the pine tree with a small caterpillar in his mouth when he spotted a familiar face waiting for him on the ground. It was his friend, Angel. Zeezoo fed the meal to one of the chicks then flew down to see what the raccoon wanted.

"Nice place you have here," said Angel. This was his first time to the tree. "And I see you have a wife and kids now. Congratulations."

"Thank you," said Zeezoo. "It's good to see you."

Angel's eyes darted around, and he lowered his voice. "Listen, Zeezoo, a situation has come up, and Shorty has called an emergency meeting of the organization. It's tonight. We need you there."

"Where will the meeting be?" asked Zeezoo. "How will I find you?"

"At dusk, I'll come for you. Do you remember where we first met by the creek? Wait for me there. And don't tell anyone. Keep this strictly hush-hush. I was never here. You understand?"

"Yes," said Zeezoo. "I understand. But what is this all about?"

"I'm not at liberty to say. My instructions were clear. Shorty said I am to personally bring you to the meeting tonight and divulge nothing. You will be apprised of the situation there."

———————

At nightfall, Angel met Zeezoo by the flat rock next to the creek then led him deeper into the woodland to a small clearing. A full moon illuminated two or three supple clouds that drifted across the heavens as well as the earth below. Toward one end of the clearing, a sawed-off tree stump jutted out of the ground. In front of it was a row of flat stones roughly six inches high, lined end to end in a small semicircle.

Zeezoo was brought to the middle stone facing the stump. "Wait here," said Angel.

The raccoon retreated to the stump and solemnly stood next to it. Bewildered, Zeezoo glanced around the clearing. No one else was there, just Angel and him. In the nearby woods, the haunting songs of lonesome crickets grew ever more wistful.

Several minutes passed. It seemed like nothing much was going to happen when abruptly Angel exclaimed, "Hear ye, hear ye, hear ye! All rise for our leader!"

Perched on the stone, Zeezoo, of course, was already standing. From out of the shadows to his right, he saw Shorty, the rat snake, slither through the grass toward the stump.

Angel stood at attention. Shorty arrived and raised his head. "Don't just stand there! Lift me up," he snapped. Angel hastily scooped Shorty's long, slender body off the ground then carefully placed him atop the stump.

Shorty looked out over the audience of one. "Now then, let's have a roll call. When I say your name, say, 'Here,'" said Shorty.

"Angel."

"Here," said Angel.

"Zeezoo."

"Here," said Zeezoo.

"Good. Good," said Shorty. "That concludes our roll call. Every-one is present. Now let's move on to the first order of business."

Zeezoo raised his wing.

"Yes, the podium recognizes comrade Zeezoo in the first row," said Shorty. "Do you wish to ask a question or make a statement?"

"Yes, sir. Thank you. I have a question, maybe two," said Zeezoo. "Are we three the only members of the organization? Also, can some-one please tell me what we're doing?"

Shorty glared at Zeezoo before answering. "Those are both good questions, my friend. This evening is a most momentous occasion for our organization. Tonight we will be welcoming a contingent of new recruits into our band of brothers, swelling our ranks. Once this is done, we will henceforth be known far and wide as 'WAR.'"

Zeezoo again raised his wing.

"Yes, comrade Zeezoo."

"What does 'WAR' mean?" he asked.

"It's an acronym for our organization," said Shorty. "It stands for 'Woodland Animals Resistance.'

"Any other questions?" asked Shorty.

Zeezoo shook his head.

"All right. Let's proceed," said Shorty. "We are deeply honored to have with us tonight a number of young men who wish to join our ranks. Angel, please escort the new recruits to our gathering so they may be formerly introduced."

"Yes, sir," said Angel. He scampered to the trees. After a minute or so, Angel returned to his position next to the tree stump with six animals of various kinds. There was a possum, porcupine, squirrel, skunk, and two small lizards that looked identical.

"Welcome! Please have a seat, men," said Shorty. The six made their way to the flat stones and sat on either side of Zeezoo.

Once they got settled, Shorty addressed them. "Thank you for coming, my friends. As you know, you each have been asked to join our organization because you possess a unique skill set that could benefit us all during times of conflict."

He then spoke to them individually. "Possum, your ability to suddenly fake your death generates confusion in the enemy. It's most impressive. Porcupine, your quills are unforgiving. Everyone fears them. Squirrel, you are the master of escape. Skunk, we all know what you're capable of. I'm glad you are with us and not against us. And lizards, you are twins—is that correct?"

"Yes, sir," the lizards answered at the same time.

"I have seen your ability to change colors and blend in with your surroundings. Your stealth is a valuable addition to the organization," said Shorty. He paused to look up at the moonlit sky. "My brothers, we stand united against those who want to destroy us and eat our young. Separately, we are weaker, and vulnerable to becoming enslaved by nature. As we well know, here in the woods, our lives and those of our beloved families are constantly at risk. This is why we have collectively formed the Woodland Animals Resistance. Resistance means standing up for our rights as living creatures. It means earning our enemy's respect. It means a pushing back against those who would do us harm."

Zeezoo, Angel, and the other animals applauded.

"Thank you. Your support is vital to our success," said Shorty. "Now then, if there's anyone here who doesn't feel up to the challenge of our cause, please leave quietly at this time. We won't judge you."

None of the six new recruits moved.

"Excellent," said Shorty. "Let me congratulate and welcome each of you to WAR, the Woodland Animals Resistance."

Zeezoo smiled. He didn't fully understand how WAR was going to achieve Shorty's vision of a safer world, but the idea of banding together with others to try to make a difference excited him. It felt right to be a part of something bigger than himself.

Shorty leaned over and whispered in Angel's ear. The raccoon again hurried off to the trees and disappeared. He returned a few moments later leading a family of five moles into the clearing. Unable to see little more than light and shadows, the five were closely huddled together, holding paws as they approached the stump.

The moles, a father and mother with their three small mole pups, came and stood next to Shorty. They stayed bunched together. The three kids clung tightly to their parents and one another, their legs trembling.

Shorty addressed the members of WAR, "Here before us now is Mr. Mole, his lovely wife, and children. I have asked them to come here this evening, so you can hear their terrifying story firsthand. I want everyone to better understand the real and present dangers we face as well as the challenges ahead of us."

Smiling warmly, Shorty turned to Mole. "The floor is yours, sir. Please tell these men what you told me earlier."

Mole stepped forward. "We need your protection," he said in a low voice. "We're helpless against him."

"And who is him?" asked Shorty. "Speak up, man."

"It's a cat," said Mole.

"What exactly happened?" asked Shorty. "Tell us in your own words. Take your time."

"Two days ago, at dawn, I was digging a new tunnel under the field next to the woods," said Mole. "Plump earthworms are plentiful around there. I never heard him coming; I was in the middle of burrowing, making good progress, when I felt the cat's paws reach in and grab me. It was my fault. I got distracted by my work."

"Don't blame yourself. It's not your fault," said Shorty. "Continue."

"He dangled me in front of his face," said Mole. "I thought for sure I was going to die and never see my family again. I begged him not to eat me."

"How did you escape?" asked Shorty.

"He held me above his open mouth. I can still feel his hot breath. I pleaded with him. I told the cat I'd do anything he wanted if he'd let me go. Finally, we struck a deal. He said he'd spare my life for that of another life. I asked him what he meant."

"What did the cat say?"

"He said he'd been searching for a bird's nest for some time, and if I gave him its exact location, he'd let me go. I told him I didn't know any birds, but I was willing to obtain the information. He said I had three days to come up with it, and if I failed, he'd return and devour me and my entire family."

"And whose nest was he looking for?"

"The cat said the nest belongs to a sparrow, someone named Zeezoo," said Mole. "I was afraid. I didn't want to die. At that moment, I would have done anything to save myself. I'm sorry. I didn't know what else to do. So I promised him I'd find the nest's location. But my three days are almost up. The cat will be coming for me and my family in the morning."

"And did you have any idea who this sparrow was before you agreed to condemn him and his loved ones to grisly deaths?" asked Shorty.

"No. I don't know him," said Mole. "But I swear to you, I had no intention of helping that cat. You have to believe me."

For a moment, an uneasy hush fell over the gathering. Shorty appeared to be thinking. Mrs. Mole was sniffling. The crickets in the woods, who'd been unusually timid since the start of the meeting, began to sing softly.

Shorty turned his attention to the gathered members of WAR. "Who among us, men, would not agree to the same terms to spare ourselves?" he asked. "What Mole did was clever. He bought himself time. But let me also say this: it is far too easy to condemn another person to death when you have never seen their face."

Again, Shorty paused before continuing, "Comrade Zeezoo, please come closer so Mr. Mole can see who you are."

Zeezoo spread his wings and fluttered closer to where Mole stood. He hovered within inches of Mole's nose then returned to his seat.

Mole hung his head. "Please forgive me."

"You didn't do anything wrong," said Zeezoo.

"Zeezoo is right," said Shorty. "But the time for apologies has passed. We need to move swiftly and devise a plan to combat this rogue cat. He must be defeated."

"What are you going to do?" asked Mole.

"I'm not sure," said Shorty. "We haven't prepared ourselves for this type of threat, and we're running out of time. We have just one night to think of something."

The new members of WAR whispered among themselves. Zeezoo raised his wing.

"Yes, comrade Zeezoo," said Shorty. "The podium again recognizes you."

The whispers stopped.

"I have an idea," said Zeezoo.

"What is it?" asked Shorty.
"Let's give the cat what he wants."

15

The somber stillness of a late-night sky gently gave way to soft blue of the predawn. As it always does, the world began to brighten, at first along the east horizon, and then, little by little, more broadly over everything.

The members of WAR took up their positions, lying in wait for Edgar to appear. A plan had been hurriedly prepared overnight, and now it was being implemented. Everyone had been given an important role and task in the group's joint defense effort, code named "Operation Save Mole."

Some thirty yards away from the entrance to Mole's underground burrow near the woods, the lizard twins were hiding together in the field's tall weeds. As they were able to change their color and blend in perfectly with the surrounding foliage, their assignment was to signal the others if and when the feline approached Mole's home.

The twins didn't have to wait long. Edgar wasted no time in returning for Mole to make good on his threat. They spotted the cat slinking silently through the field.

"Weetwoohweett, weetwoohweett!" One of the twins gave the signal, a loud repeated whistle that sounded a bit like a bird calling to its mate.

Further off in the dense woods, the others heard the signal. "The hour of reckoning has come," said Shorty. "Get ready, men."

———————————

Edgar reached the main tunnel entrance to Mole's burrow. "Your time is up, Mole. Come on out and face me," he snarled.

Scared and trembling, Mole meekly poked his head out of the dirt and squinted up at the cat. "This isn't right you know," said Mole.

"For your sake and that of your lovely family, I hope you've accomplished what I asked you to do," said Edgar. "Do you know where the sparrows' nest is?"

"Yes," said Mole. "It wasn't easy, but I got help from friends and did better than you asked."

Edgar plucked the defenseless and half-blind mole from the hole by his head, unfurled his paw, and ran a claw across Mole's neck. "Explain yourself," he said.

Mole whimpered and clasped his wide fleshy paws together as if to pray. "I captured the sparrow," he said.

"I don't believe you," said Edgar. "Right now you'd say almost anything to save your hide."

"It's true. He's my prisoner," said Mole. "I feel terrible about taking an innocent bird hostage, knowing what you intend to do to him and his babies, but you gave me no choice. I can't defend myself against you, and I'll do anything to protect and save my family."

"Where is he?" growled Edgar. "This had better not be some kind of trick."

"The sparrow is here," Mole sniveled. "Please don't hurt me. I did what you asked, cat. I can bring him out and show you."

Edgar set Mole down. "Then do it!"

Mole disappeared into his tunnel. Less than a minute later, he re-surfaced, struggling to pull a tiny rope made from strands of dried grass woven together. At the end of it was Zeezoo, the rope tied around his waist and his wings pinned behind his back. He emerged from the hole covered in dirt, coughing, his head held low.

"Wonderful!" said Edgar. "You did good, Mole."

"Does that mean I can go?" asked Mole.

"Yes," Edgar answered. "You held up your end of our deal, but you best get out of my sight before I change my mind."

Mole brought his face close to Zeezoo's. "I'm sorry, Mister Sparrow. Please forgive me. I've done an awful thing." Then Mole fled back into his burrow.

Edgar put his claw under Zeezoo's chin and forcibly raised the bird's downcast head. "Look at me!" said the cat. "Today is the day your life ends, but it's like I told you before—it's not personal. Well, maybe it is a little personal. I have a confession: I'm really going to enjoy watching you suffer."

"What are you going to do?" asked Zeezoo.

Edgar grabbed the rope that held Zeezoo. "I intend to destroy everything you care about and have you watch me do it. I'm going to eat your family. And then I'm going to eat you too."

"Please don't do this," pleaded Zeezoo.

"Here's what needs to happen. You're going to lead me to your nest," said Edgar. "If you don't, I'm going to feast not only on you but also on Mole and his loved ones."

"Leave the moles alone," said Zeezoo. "They haven't done any-thing to you. I'm begging you. Do what you want with me, but please spare them and my family."

"No dice," sneered Edgar. "Besides, it's only a matter of time before I find your nest and hatchlings. Let me ask you this, Zeezoo: why should the moles die when you have a chance to spare their innocent lives?"

"All right. You win," said Zeezoo.

He straightened himself, shook bits of dirt off his feathers, and trudged methodically toward the woods, his wings still pinned behind his back. Edgar kept pace a step or two behind, maintaining a tight hold on the rope.

When at last they reached the heavy brush and trees at the edge of woods, Zeezoo stopped. "I'm sure the cat skinner has been told about my abduction. He's my friend, and if you kill me, he's going to come for you."

"I'm not worried," said Edgar. "You made him up just to scare me off. He doesn't exist. There's no such thing as a cat skinner."

"Suit yourself," said Zeezoo. "But when you're being skinned alive and screaming in pain, don't say I didn't warn you. Be careful where you step."

Zeezoo led Edgar deep into the woodland through a dark area overgrown with tangled vines and lush plants. The dry ground turned to thick mud. With the sun still low in the morning sky, what few rays of light that were able to pierce the near-impenetrable canopy of leaves threw long glancing shadows off the surrounding forest brush.

For a larger animal like Edgar, making headway through the mire and maze of plants proved to be slow and difficult. He kept getting stuck, and his paws were covered in black sludge. Edgar yanked the rope around Zeezoo's waist in frustration. "We'd better be getting there soon," growled the cat.

Zeezoo said nothing. He had taken the cat as far away from his nest as he could. They were nearing a mature oak that had been struck by lightning and was now barely clinging to life. The tree had been badly scorched to its core, leaving a gaping wound halfway up its trunk. At some point, owls had converted the burned-out cavity into a nest. It had long since been abandoned, but remnants of the wide nest could still be seen from the ground.

"How much further?" Edgar asked angrily.

They came to a small clearing. In front of them stood the half-dead oak. Much taller than the surrounding foliage, it towered over and dominated the landscape.

With his shoulders slumped and a dejected expression, Zeezoo looked up. "There it is," he answered.

The cat dragged Zeezoo to a bush at the edge of the clearing and lashed him to one of its limbs. "I'll deal with you after I finish with your little ones," said Edgar. "In the meantime, you can watch. I hope your wife's around so I can scarf her down too."

Edgar rushed to the oak and scrambled up its side. As he neared the nest, the cat felt something pop him hard on the head. He caught a brief glimpse of the object, an acorn, as it ricocheted to the ground. Then in the next breath, a second acorn smacked him between the eyes. Then another. Suddenly a barrage of acorns was pelting him. Edgar looked up to see where they were coming from. Atop the nest, above him, was a squirrel, smiling and holding another acorn. Before he could blink, it too hurtled toward him.

"You rotten squirrel!" yelled Edgar. "I'm going to get you!" He raced up the side of the tree after it.

Squirrel bolted off the nest with the angry cat hot on his tail. He darted, dodged, and leapt from one branch to another around and around the old oak, higher and higher, with Edgar chasing after him, until he reached the far end of a thin limb with seemingly nowhere else to go.

Edgar stopped a foot or so away and carefully inched out onto the limb, his head down and claws extended. "Now I've got you. You're trapped. You're going to pay for attacking me, squirrel."

Unfortunately for Edgar, the slender limb beneath him was dead, like most of the burned oak, and too brittle to support much weight. As the cat extended a paw to try to snag Squirrel, the branch snapped. At the last possible second, Squirrel jumped and grabbed another nearby limb as Edgar plummeted to the ground.

Like most cats, Edgar was able to rotate his body in midair and land safely on his feet. Although he didn't break any bones, the sudden force of the fall when he struck the ground momentarily stunned him.

Meanwhile, the other members of WAR had untied and freed Zee-zoo. He hid himself in a low bush and watched the rest of the group's defense plan unfold.

Before Edgar was able to catch his breath and fully recover from the fall, a possum stumbled out of the surrounding brush, moaning loudly. From head to toe, his fur was covered in crushed wild blackber-ries. The berry's red juices looked like nasty bloodstains. "He's com-ing! No one is safe!" cried Possum. "Save yourself, cat! Run! Save yourself!"

"Who's coming?" asked Edgar, wide-eyed.

The possum appeared to faint, and his whole body wobbled. "It's the…the cat skinner," said Possum, gasping for breath. Then he flopped over onto his side with his tongue hanging out of his mouth and faked his untimely death.

Still a bit dazed, Edgar went over to observe the deceased possum's body. He poked at it and flipped an eyelid up to see if its eyes were dead. No movement.

From somewhere in the thick woods behind him, the cat heard a fierce growl; an animal was moving through the underbrush. He spun around. "Who is it?" Edgar called out, trembling. The hair on his back stood on end. "Show yourself!"

Suddenly, a strange-looking monster appeared from out of the brush. The beast's entire body was enveloped in thick mud, leaves, and twigs, as if it had ascended from some terrible pit. It had two hideous heads, one atop the other, both also shrouded in mud. It had the paws of a raccoon, but its upper head looked a lot like that of a snake.

"I smell you, cat!" said the creature. "It's been a long time since I've been able to catch and taste a big plump one like you."

Before Edgar had a chance to say another word, the creature rushed at him, its two heads growling loudly and arms flailing. Shrieking, the cat turned and sprinted into the nearby brush to escape, with the mud monster right behind him.

Edgar ran for his life through the mire and thick maze of plants. Soon he became entangled in thorny vines and panicked as the relentless monster tried to grab his legs. Trapped, the cat hissed and desperately looked for another way out. He spotted a sliver of daylight in the labyrinth of dense foliage that led back toward the field. Edgar bolted for it, and charged head first into the back of a porcupine.

"Hey! Watch where you're going!" said Porcupine.

A dozen or more painful quills were protruding from Edgar's face. He turned around and saw the dreaded cat skinner still hot on his heels, running and growling. To his left, Edgar spotted another narrow pathway through the muck and woods, and made a dash for it. Seconds later, he ran smack dab into a skunk.

Knocked onto his backside from the collision, Edgar looked up at the skunk. "Please, don't!" he begged, but it was too late. The skunk promptly positioned his rear end close to Edgar's face, raised his bushy tail, and sprayed the cat thoroughly.

"Hit the road, cat!" said Skunk. "You don't belong in these woods!"

With the muddy cat skinner bearing down on him, Edgar sprang to his feet and zipped past the skunk. He tore through the thick brush, but this time he didn't for a moment look back. Repeatedly, he found himself ensnared in mud and dense vegetation, but eventually he made it to the open field.

Zeezoo and the other members of WAR gathered in the early-morning shadows at the woodland's edge and watched Edgar frantically run across the field. He could be heard wailing for miles.

"Good job, men!" said Shorty.

Edgar scratched at the farmhouse door.

Cyrus refused to let him in. "How in the world did this happen?" he asked.

He grabbed a pair of pliers from his toolbox and a jug of apple cider vinegar from the pantry, and hauled the cat by the scruff of his neck to a large galvanized washbasin near the barn.

16

All was unusually quiet, even for a Sunday. The familiar sound of a train's horn crossing a highway could be heard faintly, though it was more than three miles away. The air was warm.

"Grandpa, come quick!"

Cyrus closed the gate to the chicken coop behind him and walked over to see what Terra wanted. He found her on her hands and knees beside the old garden near the house.

"Terra! Get up from there, and wash your hands," said Cyrus. "I just did a load of laundry. You're going to get your clothes dirty."

Terra stood up, brushed some loose dirt off her knees, and pointed. "Look! Some of them are alive," she said excitedly. "You said the seeds were all dead, but you were wrong. These ones want to live."

Cyrus wiped a bit of sweat off his brow and looked down. Sure enough, seven newborn corn stalks were poking their little green leafy heads up out of the soil. Despite lying in an expired seed bag for nearly a decade, these few seeds had defied the odds.

"That's amazing," said Cyrus.

"Can I plant the rest of the seeds in the bag and see if some of them want to grow too?" asked Terra.

Cyrus rubbed the stubble on his face and thought for a moment. "Sure, you can. But there are a lot of seeds in the bag. The garden needs to be cleaned up and tilled."

"Great! I'm so happy!" said Terra. She snapped a quick pic of the baby corn stalks with her phone and sent it along with a text to each of her friends.

"If you're going to be hoeing and digging in the dirt, go change your clothes. Put on something less nice that you can afford to get grubby in," said Cyrus.

Minutes later, Terra returned in different clothes. Cyrus took her in the barn to look for a spade, hoe, and shovel; they were found in a corner covered in cobwebs. A filthy pair of gloves was unearthed on a cluttered worktable. He helped her lift the heavy corn-seed bag into a wheelbarrow and brought it to the garden, which was long neglected and overrun with weeds.

Cyrus inspected the old plot for the first time in many years. It had been his wife Gracie's personal garden, a place she dearly loved to spend the day planting and working in when she was alive. If she was in the mood, she planted rows of flowers. But mostly, Gracie grew vegetables for canning and fragrant herbs, all different types depending on the season.

"Before you plant any more of these seeds, all the weeds in this garden need to be pulled out by their roots and removed," Cyrus instructed Terra. "Then you need to loosen the dirt and create a series of long rows that will help with water drainage."

Terra was excited. "I'll do a good job," she said.

"After you finish weeding the garden, come get me," said Cyrus. "I'll help you with the tilling and creating the rows. They need to be about fifteen inches apart."

He went inside the farmhouse, grabbed a half-full bottle of whiskey, and carried it with him outside, along with a glass. He sat on the front steps and watched his granddaughter struggle to weed the garden. Too many years had passed since it had last been tilled, and the weeds' roots were deep and entangled.

Cyrus took a sip, then another.

After an hour, Terra had barely made a dent, but she never stopped hoeing and tugging at the weeds.

When Cyrus woke up, he was on the ground near the barn, lying on his back. Terra stood over him, the sun high above her head, blinding him.

"Gracie?" Cyrus muttered. "Gracie, is that you?"

"No, Grandpa. It's me…Terra."

"Where am I?"

"You're with me. We're home, on the farm."

"Oh. Terra. I'm sorry. Please help me up."

Terra leaned down, put her arms around her grandpa's shoulders, and helped lift him to a sitting position. From there, despite feeling woozy, Cyrus was able to stand. At his feet lay an empty whiskey bottle.

"Are you okay?" asked Terra. "You fell down. I didn't know what to do. You looked dead, but I could tell you were breathing. I was afraid if I called an ambulance, the people at Children and Family Services would come take me away from you."

Cyrus looked her in the eyes. "I'm fine, but I must have passed out. I won't let that happen again. No one is ever going to take you away from me. I promise."

Terra put her arms around her grandpa and sobbed. After she let go, Cyrus picked up the empty bottle, walked slowly to the house, and sat back down on the front steps.

"Terra, I want you to go into the kitchen cupboards and also in my bedroom and bring me every bottle of liquor you can find," he said. "Look in the living room near my chair too. Go. Do it."

"Yes, Grandpa."

Terra disappeared into the farmhouse and returned a short while later, cradling three large bottles. She set them on the steps beside her grandfather and went back inside. A few minutes later, she came back out with two more.

"These are all the bottles that still have stuff in them," said Terra. "I found a full one under your bed."

"Go check in my truck too," said Cyrus. "Look under the seats and in the glove box."

Terra searched his truck and came back with another half-filled bottle along with two empty ones. She set them beside the others. Then she sat down beside him.

"What are you going to do?" she asked.

Cyrus grabbed one of the whiskey bottles, opened it, and leaned forward. He poured the contents on the ground next to the steps. He emptied every bottle the same way, gathered them up, and took them to a trash can beside the smokehouse. He dangled the bottles one at a time, pausing for a moment or two as if he were saying goodbye to a close friend, before letting them drop from his hand.

Afterward, he looked up and saw Terra back down on her hands and knees, tugging at a tangle of weeds in the garden. He couldn't help smile; she reminded him of his Gracie. Though still a child, Terra possessed a natural inner strength, much like her grandmother. *Where does that come from?* he wondered. He had no idea.

"Why don't you take a break, sweetheart?" said Cyrus. "I'll get this garden weeded and tilled for you. Then we'll plant the old seeds together and see if more of them want to grow."

Terra stood up and wiped her dirty hands on her pants. "Can I go check on Zeezoo and the chicks?"

"Sure, but please be careful. I don't want you falling out of the tree. And remember what I told you before. Don't touch the chicks. Mama birds don't like their babies being picked up and held."

Terra ran up to her grandpa and gave him a kiss on the cheek. "I promise not to fall," she said. "And I won't touch the babies. I just want to look at them."

She went into the barn then came back out. Then, in a flash, she was rushing across the field, singing some new song Cyrus didn't recognize.

At the base of the pine, Terra called for Zeezoo. He didn't appear to be around, but soon she spotted Elin and him flying swiftly toward her from out of a nearby bush. Zeezoo landed on Terra's shoulder. Elin, still a little unsure of the girl, came to rest on a branch close by.

"Look!" said Terra. "I've brought you some tasty snacks." She reached into her pants pocket and pulled out a handful of live mealworms.

"The chickens love these," she added. Terra dangled one of the mealworms in front of Zeezoo. He happily took the worm from her and gobbled it. "See? They're good." She placed a second worm in her palm and held it out for Elin. "It's okay. I'm not going to hurt you," said Terra. Elin cocked her head twice then flew over to Terra to retrieve the treat. She took it back to the branch and swallowed it. Before long, Terra had the mama sparrow calmly perched on her finger, eating one squirming worm after the other.

Above her, Terra heard the chicks chirping for their mother and father. *They must be hungry*, she thought. "Can I climb up and look at your babies?" she asked politely.

Zeezoo chirped twice, then Elin. Having eaten their fill, the two sparrows flew off toward the nest. Terra followed them, scrambling up the pine without much effort. She reached the hole and peered in. The five chicks had grown much larger since she'd last seen them. Their eyes were open and alert. They were no longer pink in color and naked. Their little bodies were now covered in a soft gray feathery down, with new feathers appearing on their young wings.

Despite her earlier fall and grandfather's warnings, Terra carefully retrieved her phone from a pants pocket and snapped pics of the chicks to send to her friends. All five babies were sitting up and staring at her. At first, they didn't move and stayed very quiet, but then one chirped, which instantly set them all to chirping at the same time.

Terra laughed. "I bet you'd like something to eat."

With Zeezoo and Elin looking on, she reached into her pocket and grabbed more mealworms. She dangled a worm above one of the chick's open mouths and fed it. Soon the baby sparrows were jostling one another and opening their mouths as wide as they possibly could, chirping loudly for more.

"Don't fight," said Terra, giggling. "I've got enough for everybody."

Terra made sure each of the chicks got their turn. She went from one nestling to the other until she could tell their bellies were full.

After they were fed, she stayed and studied the little sparrows. Each nestling's markings were similar but distinctive. When she examined them closely, she saw that no two birds were exactly alike. And knowing males would soon become more colorful than the females, she determined there were three boys and two girls in the nest.

Terra turned to Zeezoo, perched on a limb beside Elin not far away. "Can I give the babies their names?" she asked excitedly.

Zeezoo looked at Elin then chirped twice.

"I promise they'll be good names," said Terra.

Gazing at the five babies, she took a minute to think. The first names to pop in her head belonged to other foster kids she once knew. Terra had vowed never to forget anyone she met in foster care, but little by little, some of the memories were slipping away.

"Okay. I've got it." Terra pointed to the two girls. "You and you…your name is Arriane, and you're Beatrix."

Terra then looked at the boys and thought some more. "This is fun," she said. After another minute, she pointed again. "You're Camillo, and your name is Dian."

There was one nestling left. Terra looked at him and tried to think. He stared back at her and blinked. She laughed. "I know. I'm going to call you Skeeter," she pronounced. "I've never met anyone with that name, but you look like a Skeeter."

The nestlings looked up at Terra contentedly.

17

"Dear Lord! I can't believe my eyes," said John Perkins, owner of Perkins Tractors. "If it ain't Cyrus Kane! I haven't seen you in years."

"It's good to see you too, John," said Cyrus.

"How have you been?" asked John. "Is there anything I can do for you?"

Cyrus glanced at a long row of shiny new tractors, lined up neatly from smallest to largest outside Perkins Tractors, the area's oldest and largest agricultural and farm equipment dealer. He'd known John Perkins all his life, remembered him when he was a little boy running around the place in overalls, helping his father. Cyrus had been a friend of John's dad, Henry, before he had passed.

"I'm in the market to buy one of those," said Cyrus, pointing to the tractors. "And I'm doing well. Thanks for asking."

Together they walked over to the tractors on display. "Tell me, Cyrus. When was the last time you bought a tractor?" asked John.

"Thirty to forty years ago," answered Cyrus.

John laughed. "Well, you're in for a bit of a shock. These tractors today aren't like the old ones you drove as a boy. The ones you're staring at are high-tech agricultural machines with satellite guidance and computer systems that do a lot of the thinking for you. They have touch-screen displays synced with built-in wireless technology that simplify every aspect of the planting process—from field preparation to seed placement and fertilization, right through harvest."

"You know, I'm old school," said Cyrus. "I'm not ready for all this new stuff. Don't you have a few used tractors for sale that don't have all this fancy gadgetry?"

"Listen. It's simple," said John. "If you know how to touch a screen with your finger, you can do it. There's no reason to return to the antiquated ways of doing things. The computer software and system will save you time and money and improve the quality of your crops."

"I'm not sure," said Cyrus. "I don't think I'm ready to join this new computerized world you're talking about. I'd prefer to keep things uncomplicated, the way I'm used to."

John walked Cyrus over to the second-largest tractor in the row and placed his hand on one of its front tires. "I know the size of your farm, and this tractor is ideal for what you need. It comes with all the bells and whistles I talked about. And best of all, it has an enclosed air-conditioned cab."

"Air conditioning?" Cyrus looked up at the tractor, its paint job gleaming in the sun.

"Yes, air conditioning," repeated John.

"How soon can you deliver it?"

"Tomorrow morning."

It had only been a day since Cyrus had vowed to never drink again, but already, he felt revitalized. As he left Perkins Tractors, he thought, *I don't want to be numb to life anymore.*

He stopped by the feed store to pick up more food for the animals. While there, he had the truck loaded down with a half-dozen fifty-pound bags of corn seed. He made arrangements for another twenty bags of seed to be delivered to the farm. He then drove to a roofing-supply company and bought new shingles for the barn. Its leaky roof had been neglected far too long. The barn, chicken coop, shed, pens, and entire surroundings needed to be cleaned up and organized.

Cyrus' final stop was to the hardware store, where he bought work gloves, nails, tape, sandpaper, and a few other essentials. By the time he got back in his truck, it was nearly time for Terra's school to let out. Since he was in town already, he made a last-minute decision to swing by and pick her up before she got on the bus.

He pulled into the school's parking lot and waited beside the truck. He timed his arrival well. After the bell rang, swarms of children poured out of the building. He spotted his granddaughter noisily conversing with three other girls. They were headed to the buses lined up end to end in the pick-up area.

"Hey, Terra!" shouted Cyrus. "Over here!"

Terra raised her head. She waved to her grandpa and ran over. "Why are you here?"

"I was in the area and finished what I was doing. I thought maybe we'd go home together," answered Cyrus.

Terra took off her backpack and tossed it into the truck bed. "What's all this stuff?" she asked.

"I've decided it's time I cleaned up a few things around the farm," said Cyrus. "These are corn seeds for our new crop this year. And these are materials to redo the roof on the barn. I'm having new shingles delivered, and I bought a new tractor."

"Wow! I can't wait to see it," said Terra. "Are you going to let me ride on the tractor with you?"

"Of course, and if you want, I can teach you how to drive it. But you need to grow a couple of inches taller before you can maneuver it safely by yourself. How does that sound?"

"Sounds awesome!" said Terra.

"Well, get in," said Cyrus. He looked up. The clouds were starting to turn a darker shade of gray. "I need to unload everything into the barn before it rains."

Terra ran around to the passenger side and opened the door. Cyrus reached into the truck bed to make sure there was nothing loose that might accidentally bounce free and fall out on the ride home. After better securing a few things, he looked up. Terra stood four or five feet away from him. Behind her was a man. He had a firm grip on Terra's arm and a gun pointed at her head.

"What the…?" said Cyrus. "What is this?"

"Your granddaughter knows why I'm here," said the stranger. "Don't you, Terra?"

"Grandpa, I'm scared."

"Who the hell are you?" asked Cyrus. His first instinct was to lunge at the man, but he'd risk the gun going off. Cyrus' voice trembled as he balled his hands into fists.

"My name's Stanislav," the man answered. "And you're Cyrus Kane. It took me a while to find you. Finding where Terra went to school was easy, but you—"

"What do you want?" asked Cyrus, interrupting, his voice tense and angry.

"Your daughter, Mary, stole money from me," said Stanislav. He tightened his hold on Terra and brought the barrel of his gun to the small of her back. He quickly looked around. Several mothers and fathers were in the vicinity, still picking up their kids. "If either of you raises your voice or tries to draw attention, I won't hesitate to shoot Terra. So I strongly suggest you both stay calm and listen up."

Cyrus glared at Stanislav. "Tell me. What do you want?" he repeated.

"I want my money," said Stanislav. "And in exchange, I promise not to kill Mary."

"Where is she?" asked Cyrus. "What have you done with her?"

"Relax. She's fine for now. Mary has some ugly bruises and a black eye," answered Stanislav. "When we found her, she didn't have the money and wasn't exactly forthcoming on who might pay off her debt. It took a little while to learn she had a father in the area."

"My mom didn't steal the money," blurted Terra. "I did it. When she paid you back, you tried to rip her off. I saw how you took advantage of her because she gets weak for your stupid pills."

"I'm not surprised—like mother, like daughter. You simple-minded brat. I'm sure you'll end up just like your mom, a worthless drug addict and thief," said Stanislav.

"Shut up," said Cyrus. "Don't talk to her like that."

"Or what?" Stanislav cocked the gun. "What are you going to do?"

Cyrus opened his palms and quickly raised his hands. "Okay. Okay...Take it easy," he said. "What do you want?"

"I want the money your daughter stole from me!" repeated Stanislav.

"How much does she owe you?" asked Cyrus. He thought about distracting Stanislav, rushing at his legs and tackling him hard to the ground before the guy had a chance to fire a shot, but Terra stood between the gun and him. Cyrus dared not risk it.

"Twenty thousand dollars," said Stanislav. "You've got one day. If I don't have the money, every penny of it by nine p.m. tomorrow, you can say goodbye to Mary forever."

"You're a liar!" cried Terra. "You said my mom only owed you five thousand."

Stanislav yanked her arm. "If you don't want a bullet in you, you'll stay quiet," he growled. "Five thousand was yesterday. You're lucky I'm not asking for fifty thousand. If you ask me, your mom's not worth five cents. So I'm being more than fair, considering."

"What if I can't come up with the money?" asked Cyrus.

"That's your problem," said Stanislav. "Now listen closely. I'm going to drop an envelope on the ground. There's a note inside with instructions on where to leave the cash. If you do exactly what you're told, I'll release Mary. But if you stupidly decide to go to the cops or anyone else, I won't hesitate to bury her where you'll never find her body. The choice is yours."

"How do we know you haven't killed her already?" asked Cyrus. "We need to know she's alive and safe."

"In the envelope is a photo taken today," answered Stanislav. "Let's not make this complicated, Mr. Kane. I have bosses who expect me to make good on the money. You simply do what I tell you to do, and everything will be fine. But if this doesn't go down the way I want, know this: I won't stop with Mary. I'll be back for Terra next. Understood?"

"Yes," said Cyrus.

The two men glared at each other. Nothing more was said. Stanislav kept his gun raised but let go of Terra. He reached into his pocket, pulled out an envelope, and tossed it down. Then, from seemingly out of nowhere, a large black SUV sped toward them and abruptly stopped behind Stanislav.

The unknown male driver's features were concealed behind black-tinted windows and dark sunglasses, but his voice was distinct. "Get in!" he yelled. Stanislav quickly jumped into the SUV. Tires screeching, they sped away.

Terra ran after the SUV, trying to read its license plate number, but by then it was too far away. Cyrus rushed to his granddaughter and held her.

"What are we going to do?" asked Terra.

"Find your mom," he answered.

Roberta Johnson returned to her desk with a cream-cheese Danish and can of orange soda. She handed them to Terra before sitting back down.

"Here you go, dear," she said. "It's all I could find in the break-room. The staff around here are like vultures. If there's even a hint of cake, cookies, or some other sweet thing, they devour it. By this time of day, everything's usually gone. That was the last Danish."

"Thank you," said Terra. "But I'm not very hungry."

"Here are the original copies of the ransom note and the photo of Mary," Roberta said. She handed them to Cyrus, who was sitting next to Terra. "I've scanned the note and photo into our computer system and also have forwarded copies to the police."

"We weren't sure where to go," said Cyrus, who kept squinting. The fluorescent overhead lights in Roberta's office bothered his eyes.

He glanced at his granddaughter. She was pulling apart small chunks and nibbling on the Danish.

"Given the threat, you did the right thing by coming here," Roberta said. "We can't know for sure if this Stanislav guy has a way of monitoring who comes and goes at the police station."

"We greatly appreciate all your help," said Cyrus.

"I've emailed to the police your description of Stanislav as well as Terra's description regarding where he lives. Based on her recollection of the area and details on how she got there, they think they have a good idea which apartment building her mother took her to. They say a detective will be stopping by the farm first thing in the morning."

"We'll be on the lookout then," said Cyrus. He stood up. "Finish it up, Terra, or bring what's left with you. Let's get home."

Roberta reached into a drawer for one of her business cards. She scribbled something on the back of it and handed it to Cyrus. "Here's the cell number for Detective Bradbury. He's been assigned the lead investigator on this case. If you have questions or there's an emergency, or if you have more information that might help, don't hesitate to call him. I'll assist you the best I can as well."

Cyrus and Terra thanked Roberta and left. Outside, the weather had turned even more blustery than earlier. Scraps of littered paper and a plastic bag with the words "Thank You for Shopping at Piggles" twirled and tumbled down the sidewalk.

They jumped into the truck and headed for home. On the outskirts of town, a short-lived cloudburst opened up above them. The fierce torrent of rain came down so hard that it was difficult to see out the windshield, but less than two minutes later, it was gone, leaving the asphalt road ahead glistening.

Further on, Cyrus came to a four-way stop at a rural crossroads. An old gas station and country store, long abandoned and crumbling, stood on one corner. Two freshly plowed farm fields and an undeveloped, densely-wooded plot made up the remaining three dissected corners. Over the years, he had passed by this place thousands of times on his way to and from the farm. To the left was the way back home. He looked at Terra, thought for a moment, and turned right.

"Where are you going?" asked Terra.

"I need to show you something," said Cyrus.

He drove several miles, turning down two narrow backroads until he reached a desolate unpaved drive across from a small white chapel. He turned in and drove another quarter mile. At the end of it was a field of grass, dotted by a smattering of gravestones and tall centuries-old oaks.

"Have you ever been here?" asked Cyrus.

"No," said Terra. "I've never seen this place."

Cyrus parked the truck and got out. Terra followed him as he walked quietly through the cemetery. No one else was around. Sparse rows of granite and marble headstones extended across a slightly rolling landscape of not more than an acre. Two squirrels were chasing each other up an oak. An inquisitive blue jay landed on a nearby headstone and cocked its head.

At a small flat gray stone, Cyrus knelt and brushed away a few stray leaves and a bit of dirt. Above the stone was a vase that held a single plastic red rose. He bowed his head and closed his eyes in silent prayer. He then stood up and wiped the grass off his pants.

"This is where your grandmother lies," said Cyrus. "You never met her, but she was a wonderful person. Both of you would have gotten along well. I loved her deeply."

"I've only seen the pictures of her that you showed me," said Terra. "She looked nice."

"She was," said Cyrus, "in every way. Grace had a loving heart, just like you. When she died, I lost a big part of me. She was the best thing that ever happened to me. I miss her terribly."

Cyrus reached out and took Terra's hand. He then led her to another part of the cemetery. The leaves on the oaks could be heard rustling in the wind. A second blue jay landed on a stone near the first one.

He stopped in front of a modest military gravestone fashioned out of white marble. The name engraved on it was Victor Delarosa, Terra's father. Etched above his name was the outline of a simple cross, and below it, the words PFC, AFGHANISTAN. Beneath that were the dates memorializing his birth and death, and lastly near the bottom, it read, LOVING HUSBAND AND FATHER.

At first, Terra said nothing. Expressionless, she stared at the simple marker. But after a long pause in which Cyrus felt like the earth itself had stopped turning, she reached out and touched her father's name, tenderly tracing her fingers over it.

"I don't remember him," said Terra softly.

"You were just a baby when he passed," said Cyrus.

A small American flag on a stick had been placed in the ground next to the stone. Faded and worn, its stars and stripes waved briskly when a sudden gust of wind swirled then went limp as it subsided.

"Where is Afghanistan?" asked Terra.

"On the other side of the world. It's a dry place with deserts and mountains, where war seems to go on and on forever. Men have conquered and fought over the land there for a thousand years."

"It took my daddy away from me," said Terra. "And I hate it. I hate it!"

Cyrus put his hand on Terra's shoulder. The flag fluttered in the wind for a moment then fell again.

"Tell me," said Terra. "What was my dad like?"

"Before he went off to war, he was a good person, kind and considerate. He loved you very much." Cyrus hesitated to say more, but Terra needed to know the entire truth, not just part of it. "But your dad came back a different man," he added. "He wasn't the same guy he was before they sent him to Afghanistan."

"But...I thought my dad died in Afghanistan," said Terra. "Mom said he got blown up by a bomb when he drove over it with his army truck. He never came back to us...not alive. She told me he died while he was over there helping other people be free."

"That's not true," said Cyrus. "After he was discharged from the army, he came back home to you and your mom very much alive. But the war and the bad things he experienced there—the buddies and civilians he saw die right in front of him—it all changed him. When your dad returned, he suffered from depression and was more withdrawn from the people he loved. He'd often sit in a room and stare at nothing for days on end. Have you heard of PTSD? Do you know what that is?"

"No," said Terra.

"PTSD stands for 'post-traumatic stress disorder.' It's a mental health condition that's common among soldiers returning from war."

Under a nearby oak, there was a stone bench. Cyrus led Terra to it. The bench had a quote engraved on its seat that read, THOSE WE HAVE HELD IN OUR ARMS FOR A LITTLE WHILE, WE HOLD IN OUR HEARTS FOREVER.

They sat down, and Cyrus continued. "Because he suffered from PTSD, your father often thought he was still fighting in the war. He would have nightmares and wake up in bed shouting. Sometimes he had hallucinations where he believed the enemy was attacking him. We tried to get him admitted into a veterans medical center for treatment and to keep him safe, but there was a waiting list. We never got a straight answer as to how long it was going to take, maybe years. The doctors prescribed him all kinds of medicines to keep him calm, but they didn't work, and it was never enough. So he bought illegal drugs on the street."

"But my dad is dead," Terra interrupted, her eyes focused on her grandfather. "How did he die?"

"I'm the reason he's here," said Cyrus. "I killed him."

There was a fleeting respite of silence.

"I don't understand! Why?" cried Terra. She stood up. "Why did you do it?"

Cyrus lowered his head and looked away. "Your mother called me. It was after midnight. She would contact me instead of the police when your dad became violent, because she didn't want him to be arrested," he said softly. "She was frantic on the phone. I showed up, and Victor was in a complete rage, yelling nonsense. He was out of his mind. Normally I could simply talk to him and he'd eventually calm down, but this time…this time was different. I can't say for sure, but maybe the combination of prescribed medications he was given mixed with illegal drugs made things worse. And maybe the drugs didn't have anything to do with it. Maybe he just snapped."

He looked up at his granddaughter. "He had bloodied your mother's face before I arrived. It wasn't the first time he'd beaten her. She was cowering in a corner of the room, holding you in her arms. You were just a toddler in diapers. Victor kept accusing her of being a spy for the Taliban, an enemy militia in Afghanistan. He went into the bedroom, and when he came out, he held a handgun. He pointed it at her head. I was close enough to grab his arm, and I wrestled him to the floor. He fought me, but I managed to get the gun away from him."

The two squirrels were back on the ground, chasing each other through rows of headstones. A truck pulled up near the cemetery. Two slow-moving workers got out. They grabbed shovels and a roll of green tarp.

"No one ever told me about this," said Terra. "I can't understand why my dad did that. Why would he beat Mom? What happened to him? Why was he so crazy?"

"It was the damn war," said Cyrus. "Maybe a bomb didn't kill him like you were told, but he came back home more dead inside than alive. It was seeing all the insanity and destruction of people—man's inhumanity to his fellow man—that killed him. They killed his faith. They killed the hope inside his soul, and when you kill all the hope in a man, he might as well be dead."

"Why did you kill him?"

"Your dad ran off into the kitchen. I heard him talking to himself. Your mom had deep bruises all over her arms and face and was bleeding badly. She needed to go to the hospital. She had a deep cut above her eye. I told her to call 911, but she refused. I grabbed a towel from the bathroom and was trying to stop the bleeding. I was putting pressure on the wound and telling her to leave with me. You both needed to get away from him. Suddenly, she screamed. I spun around and Victor was holding a butcher knife. He came at me, and I pulled the trigger."

Terra said nothing.

"Your mother never forgave me," said Cyrus. "She blames me for your father's death. To this day, I'm not sure I did the right thing. Maybe there was a chance I could have reasoned with him or grabbed his arm and took away the knife. In my mind, I've played out that moment again and again a thousand times, and it doesn't change a thing. In the end I lost everything that mattered. I lost my daughter…and I lost you."

There was another long silence. The two workers were on the far side of the cemetery. They had finished stacking a pile of metal chairs on the grass beside the tarp and shovels and were on their knees across from each other, reading a tape measure.

"Can we go home now?" asked Terra.

"Sure. It's been a long day."

Cyrus wanted to cry, but he was able to hold off the flow of tears until they were back on the farm. He went for a walk behind the barn.

18

A damp early fog enveloped the entire farm. The old rusted tractor, barn, garden, and fields—everything in the distance—lay buried in a blanket of soft white mist. Cyrus stepped outside and yawned. He needed to check on Lizzie's bad leg. She'd been limping a little more lately.

Cyrus walked through the haze to the barn. On his way, he heard Terra giggling. He took a quick peek out back. His granddaughter was already up and in the goat pen, filling their trough with fresh water from a hose. Thor and Loki were playfully nudging Terra's hands, trying to entice her to rub and scratch their heads.

Lizzie's leg appeared to be all right. There was no new damage that Cyrus could feel. He brushed her down and gave her some oats. He had to face the truth. The mare had lived a lot longer than most horses do, and the end wasn't far off. Maybe she had a year or two more. He needed to call a veterinarian and have a full health exam done on her.

Engrossed in tending to Lizzie, Cyrus never heard the car's approach on the dirt road. From somewhere behind him inside the barn, a man's voice called out, "Is anyone home?"

Terra rushed in. "Someone's here," she said.

Cyrus patted Lizzie and closed the stall door behind him. A tall trim man in a dark-blue suit stood in the middle of the barn. He held a folder and computer tablet. When he saw Cyrus and Terra, he extended his arm warmly and shook their hands. "You two must be Cyrus Kane and Terra Delarosa," he said.

"Yes," answered Cyrus. "I take it you're Detective Bradbury."

Detective Bradbury removed a wallet from his inside coat pocket and flashed his photo ID and badge. When his suit coat parted, a large revolver in a black leather holster attached to his belt was briefly exposed.

"I grew up on a farm," said Detective Bradbury. He glanced around. "The look and smell of this place bring back fond memories."

"Where's your family's farm?" asked Cyrus.

"It was on the other side of the county, but it's gone now," the detective answered. "My folks had several bad years in a row, and when they couldn't pay their bills, they borrowed heavily. You can guess the rest. The bank foreclosed and took their farm."

"I'm sorry," said Cyrus.

"Well, the past is dead and never coming back," said Detective Bradbury. "All any of us can do is learn from our mistakes and concentrate on fixing the things we still have some control over."

Detective Bradbury looked down at his tablet, tapped a few touchscreen keys, and pulled up a photograph. He held out the computer screen to show Terra. The photo was a mug shot of a rugged man with dark eyes, thick black hair, and a goatee. He glared menacingly at the camera.

"Is this the man you saw the day you were with your mother and the one who assaulted you with a gun yesterday?" asked Detective Bradbury.

"Yes. That's him," said Terra.

"His name is Stanislav Sobakin," said Detective Bradbury. "He's been on our radar for some time. In the recent past, he's been picked up for possession of illegal drugs and passing counterfeit money. We think he's part of a larger crime syndicate, but we haven't been able to pin anything more on him yet."

Detective Bradbury tapped a few more keys. Another file photograph popped up of a tall building. Terra recognized it immediately.

"That's where my mom took me," said Terra.

"We sent an undercover officer to the apartment on the fifth floor last night, pretending to be a strung-out drug buyer," said Detective Bradbury. "But Stanislav wasn't there. The officer got a good look around. The two women there claimed they don't know him."

"Maybe Stanislav does his business there regularly and comes and goes," said Cyrus. "If he returns, you could arrest him and make him tell you where he's keeping Mary."

"You might be right," said Detective Bradbury. "But unfortunately, our violent crimes unit is backlogged with too many cases. We're understaffed and don't have the resources to stake out a location all day long. My guess is Stanislav is lying low for a while or has moved his operation somewhere else. We have a team in place working to find leads on where he is."

"Is there anything we can do to help?" asked Cyrus.

"For the time being, it's important you both stay calm and don't do anything. Given how brazen Stanislav was yesterday, Terra clearly needs to stay home from school until this is resolved. Ms. Johnson will inform the principal of the situation. I've got your cell number, Mr. Kane, and I'll stay in touch. But before I go, I want to discuss the ransom money that Stanislav wants and this photograph of Mary."

"He wants me to bring twenty thousand dollars in cash—twenty-dollar bills—and leave it in a grocery bag ten paces behind the nearest speed limit sign from our farm. It's the fifty-five-mile-an-hour sign about a half mile from here headed toward town," said Cyrus.

"Have you withdrawn the money yet?" asked Detective Bradbury.

"No. I'm going to the bank this morning to get it," answered Cyrus. He glanced at Terra, who was listening intently to the conversation.

"All right, that's fine," said Detective Bradbury. "Do it first thing this morning. If we're unable to find Stanislav, you might have no choice but to capitulate and give him what he wants. He won't release Mary until after he has the money, so we'll need to stay out of sight and try to follow him from the drop-off location to where he's keeping her." He paused to pull up another file on his tablet. "After you go to the bank, bring the money to the police station, and we'll swap your cash for marked bills. If he succeeds in getting away with the money, we'll be able to trace the bills later."

"What if he gets all the money and kills my mom anyway?" interrupted Terra. "Stanislav is a liar, and I don't trust him to keep his promise."

Detective Bradbury looked Terra in the eyes. He didn't mince his words. "You're smart not to believe him," he responded calmly. "I know it's difficult, but please trust us to handle things. We'll advise you and your grandfather regarding what steps to take next, so the outcome is positive. I'm not in the business of making promises I can't keep, but rest assured, we'll work hard to make sure your mother is returned to you safe and sound."

He turned the screen around to show Cyrus and Terra the photograph of Mary that Stanislav had left in the envelope. It was a full-length shot of her tied to a wooden chair, her hands tied behind her back. She was staring back at the camera, disheveled and sweaty. Her face was bruised and swollen, her eye blackened.

"Do either of you recognize the room that this photo was taken in?" asked the detective.

Behind Mary was an olive green wall, to her right, a small wooden side table and, on it, a lamp with a white shade above a brownish hourglass-shaped base. Over her left shoulder, sunlight streamed brightly through a window. Someone had pulled back beige curtains that had a colorful flower pattern running down the folds.

"I don't recognize it," said Cyrus. "Do you, Terra?"

Terra studied the room in the photo intently. "No. I don't know where this is. But what is this out the window? There's like a word in the sky."

"Where do you see it?" asked Detective Bradbury.

She pointed to a faint string of red shapes beyond the window in the photo. They appeared to be no more than tiny squiggles softened and bleached by the sunlight surrounding them.

"It's right there. Don't you see the word?" said Terra. "There's an 'n.' That one is a 'c,' and then this one is a 'y.'"

Detective Bradbury looked more closely. "Yes. I see them now. I can barely make them out, but you're right. Those are three tiny letters. They spell 'ncy.' They might be part of a billboard or road sign of some sort."

"What does 'ncy' mean?" asked Terra.

"I'm really not sure," answered the detective. "It's clearly just the last part of a word or name, possibly 'agency' or 'Nancy.' I'm not sure that makes any sense."

"Vacancy!" said Cyrus. "The word is 'vacancy.' That explains why the letters are red. It's a neon vacancy sign on a street or highway.

Mary's being held at some short-term rental apartment or maybe a motel."

"The decorations in the room look very dated," added Detective Bradbury. "I think you're right. Stanislav is likely holding her at some older motel or weekly rental in the area, possibly a house or apartment. Thank you, Terra. We'll send out a dispatch this morning to the officers on patrol and start looking for vacancy signs. Hopefully this will lead us to your mother."

"Can you text me the photo of my mom?" asked Terra. "I'd like to have a copy of it."

"Sure, I can," answered the detective. "I'll also send one to your grandfather's phone. Maybe it'll jog a memory or help you find more clues as to where your mother is." He touched several keys on the screen, and it was done.

"What's next?" asked Cyrus.

"After you swap your cash at the station for marked bills, come back home, and wait for me to contact you. Stanislav has given you until nine p.m. tonight. Let's see how this plays out. Our top priority is to find Mary. If that fails, we could try to hide a GPS tracking device in the bag with the ransom money, but if Stanislav were to find it, he might follow through on his threat. I'll be blunt: this guy is dangerous. Planting a tracker on him is too big a risk."

"I understand," said Cyrus.

They shook hands. Detective Bradbury told Terra not to worry and politely said goodbye. He went to his car, backed up, and left. The fog was beginning to lift.

Once the detective was out of sight, Cyrus turned to Terra. "I want you to go to the woods and find Zeezoo. Tell him we need his help," he said.

19

Outside the police station, Terra waited in the truck with Zeezoo for her grandfather's return. She retrieved the photo of her mother on her phone and held it up for the sparrow to see.

"Here. This is what my mom looks like," said Terra.

Perched atop the steering wheel, Zeezoo cocked his head and studied the image.

"She's done some wrong things and had to go to jail," Terra continued. "But I know deep inside my mom's a good person. She has a drug problem. And now a bad guy says he's going to hurt her or maybe kill her. We need to find my mom before that happens."

Having lost his own mother when he was a newborn chick, Zeezoo felt Terra's anguish over the possibility of losing her mom to whoever this Stanislav was. He flew to her shoulder and gave her a peck on the cheek to show he understood.

"Grandpa told me how he found you on the ground and that he couldn't find your mom," said Terra. "I'm sure you felt bad about it, Zeezoo. Your mother must have loved you a lot, and I don't

145

know…maybe your mom saved you so you could live long and be happy. I wish I could go back in time and bring her to you."

Terra paused for a moment to watch a well-dressed young couple walking by on the sidewalk. They were holding hands, their faces smiling. A half block away, they crossed the street and turned to walk up the steps into the courthouse.

"No matter what she does, I know my mom loves me," Terra added.

Cyrus emerged from the police station soon after, holding the same bag he'd gone in with. He wore a look of concern when he stepped into the truck and got behind the wheel.

"Did they give you the new money?" asked Terra.

"Yes. It's all here," he answered.

Cyrus pulled out one of the banded stacks of twenty-dollar bills and briefly showed it to Terra. He then put the stack back in with the rest and shoved the bag full of money under the driver's seat.

"We have a total of forty banded twenty-dollar stacks, twenty-five bills in each stack," he added. "The police have entered the serial numbers on these bills into a database. The bills also have been stamped with UV-visible ink so they can be traced."

"What are we going to do now?" asked Terra. "Are we going back home to wait, like Detective Bradbury told us to do?"

Cyrus seemed to be staring into space. "I've lived around here all my life, and I know where most every motel is." He was muttering quietly under his breath to himself. "There's also a chance Stanislav is holding Mary in some apartment you can rent on the cheap for just the day or week. A room like that will be difficult to locate. The only real clue we have is the neon sign."

"What are you thinking, Grandpa?"

He paused and rubbed his chin. "Rather than sit and wait for the police to contact us, we should drive by a few of the older mom-and-pop motels and see if any of them still have a large NO VACANCY sign out front," said Cyrus. "I've got an idea as to how we can look for Mary safely. Zeezoo can help us."

Cyrus drove from one end of town to the other, searching for aging motels and apartment buildings with an old-style neon vacancy sign out front. He kept a lookout on the left-hand side while Terra and Zeezoo scouted the right, but nothing turned up. Most of the motels Cyrus remembered had been renovated at some point in the past. Several places still had their original roadside signs up, but the neon lights had been dismantled and removed. On one sign, the words NO VACANCY had been blackened out with paint.

"What are the vacancy signs for?" asked Terra.

"Believe it or not, there was a time when personal computers, cell phones, and the Internet didn't exist," explained Cyrus. "Back in the day, they used them to let travelers know whether they had any rooms available. Let's say you were driving on a vacation or maybe a business trip, and you were tired and ready to stop somewhere for the night to sleep. If you saw NO lit up in bright red, it meant the motel was full. And if just VACANCY was lit, it was an invitation to stop in because every room wasn't taken yet."

With the window rolled down so she could see better, Terra kept her eyes fixed on the buildings and homes. After a while, everything began to look the same. The world of structures and signs was becoming a blur. She preferred to watch the people coming and going, the postal worker delivering the mail, the chubby man walking two small dogs. She spotted a striped black-and-white cat sitting atop a fence. It reminded her of Edgar.

"But what if we don't find where Stanislav's keeping Mom?" she asked. "What are we going to do?"

"We'll have no choice but to give him the ransom money and hope he keeps his promise. But like you said, he can't be trusted. What we're doing is a long shot. She might be close by or a thousand miles away. There's no way to know. But my guess is Stanislav is lazy. It's why he's a drug pusher and a thief. So he probably didn't take your mom far."

Terra started to say something when Zeezoo suddenly leapt out the window of the moving truck and flew away. She caught a glimpse of him darting off, but in seconds, his tiny figure disappeared.

"Stop!" yelled Terra. "Zeezoo's gone!"

Cyrus slammed on the brakes and brought the truck to a stop. He looked over his shoulder and also in the rearview mirror to see if he could spot the sparrow. "Did you see which way he went?" he asked.

"He flew down the street we just passed…on my side," said Terra. "But I lost sight of him." She was on the verge of tears at the thought of losing her friend.

Cyrus tried to calm her. "Don't worry. Zeezoo is smart. He knows his way home. I'll turn around and see if we can find him."

He made a U-turn at the next intersection and sped back to the cross street they'd just passed. He turned and raced down it. Toward the end of the block on the left, Terra spotted Zeezoo. Pointing, she shouted, "There he is!"

Zeezoo was perched atop a huge mustard-colored 1950's era sign. Written in cursive blue neon light were the words MOTEL MARS. Higher above the sign was an illuminated white arrow, pointing toward the motel, and beneath it all on a separate smaller sign, in bright-red neon letters, it said, NO VACANCY.

"That's amazing," said Cyrus. "I'll never figure out how Zeezoo is able to understand what we're saying, but he does. I'd forgotten about this place."

Cyrus pulled over next to the curb directly across the street from the Motel Mars and whistled. Zeezoo came flying back to them and landed on Terra's lap.

"You did good, Zeezoo," said Terra. "But next time, please warn me before you go flying off somewhere by yourself. Okay?"

Zeezoo looked up and chirped twice.

Motel Mars had a sad look of neglect. The run-down two-story building with ten rooms facing the street on each floor was in a state of disrepair. Cardboard boxes and large trash bags were tossed about on the walkway outside several doors. Parts of a dismantled crib leaned against a wall. A beat-up car with its hood up and a flat tire was parked in front of one of the rooms.

Cyrus nudged his granddaughter. "Hey, take a look over there."

To the right, backed into a parking space near the stairs at the end of the building, was the black SUV with tinted windows that had raced into the parking lot and picked up Stanislav at Terra's school.

"Does Zeezoo know what Mary looks like?" asked Cyrus. "We need to know if she's being held in one of the rooms without drawing attention to ourselves."

"Yes. I showed him the picture of my mom," said Terra.

"Good. If that's the same vehicle we saw Stanislav get in yester-day, he might be holding her in one of the units over on that end of the building. People typically park close to the room they paid for."

"Shouldn't we call Detective Bradbury and let him know?" asked Terra.

"Not yet. He told us to stay out of his way, and we don't know for sure if Mary is even here. This is why I brought Zeezoo along. Listen, Zeezoo. We need you to fly to those windows over there and peek inside. If Terra's mother is being held in one of the rooms, chirp twice. We'll be watching. Can you do that for us?"

Zeezoo chirped twice and leapt out the window. He flew to the old motel and began his search along the first floor. Cyrus and Terra watched him land on a windowsill. He spent less than a minute there peering inside before fluttering off to the next room and on down the line. He bypassed windows with closed curtains for ones that were open, until he came to the last room on the end of the upper floor, located directly above where the black SUV was parked.

The curtains on its windows were closed, but Zeezoo was slow to leave. Hopping back and forth along the sill, he appeared to be very interested in something. He cocked his head and fluffed his feathers. He then flew away momentarily, only to circle around and return to the same spot by the window.

"I think he hears someone inside," said Cyrus.

They watched Zeezoo flutter above the sill and bang against the window with his feet and body. He did this several times. The curtain opened. Someone behind the glass wanted to see who or what was making all the commotion. Then the signal came: two quick chirps.

Cyrus opened the glove box and pulled out a baseball cap and sunglasses. "Wait here," he said. "And promise me. Whatever you do, Terra, keep the doors locked, and don't leave this truck. If I'm not back in ten minutes, call the detective."

"What are you going to do?" asked Terra.

"I'm not exactly sure," answered Cyrus, "but I'll figure it out."

Putting on the sunglasses and pulling the brim of the cap down lower over his eyes, Cyrus crossed the street and the Motel Mars parking lot. He took the stairs to the second floor and knocked on the door.

From inside, he heard a man ask, "Who is it?"

It was the same distinctive male voice from the day before, the person behind the wheel of the black SUV who was working with Stanislav.

"I'm with maintenance," said Cyrus. "I've come to fix the leaky plumbing in the bathroom."

The response from inside was swift and threatening. "There's nothing wrong with the plumbing. So I suggest you get lost!"

Cyrus waited for a moment then beat on the door harder. "I'm sorry, but if I don't fix the leak, they'll fire me and get someone else. You need to let me in."

He heard whispering and brief movement inside. The door cracked open, and a heavyset man leaned his face out. He had a shaved head and a large tattoo on his neck. "What the hell's the matter with you?" he said loudly. "There's no leak. I told you to go away!"

"Not today!" said Cyrus. He punched the man in the face with everything he had and shoved him back in the room. Stunned by the unexpected blow, the man fell hard. Cyrus scanned the room. Mary was strapped to a chair, her mouth gagged. A large revolver lay on a table. The man struggled to get up with Cyrus on top of his body, beating him bloody with his fists. He grabbed hold of Cyrus' shirt and tossed him aside. They both rose to their feet.

Rushing at Cyrus with fists raised, the man snarled, "Who are you?"

The heavyset man swung wildly and missed. Cyrus answered with a vicious punch that landed squarely on the guy's nose. It dazed him, and he stumbled backward but kept to his feet. Cyrus grabbed a lamp off an end table, yanked its plug from the wall, and cracked it hard over the man's head. He fell to the floor and lay there, unconscious from the blow.

"I'm the son of a bitch who wants his daughter back," said Cyrus. He was out of breath and bleeding a bit. He rushed to Mary. "Let's get you out of here."

Cyrus removed Mary's gag and untied her arms and legs. Her face was badly bruised, clothes torn. Weak from the ordeal, she had a difficult time standing. He put his arms around her to help support her weight.

"How did you find me?" asked Mary.

"With the help of your daughter and that little guy over there," said Cyrus.

Zeezoo had flown into the room and was atop the motionless man on the floor, pecking away at his bald head.

"Get off him," Cyrus told the bird. "You might wake the guy up. We need to leave quickly."

Her arms draped loosely around his neck, Cyrus lifted Mary and carried her out the door. It was time to contact Detective Bradbury. Cyrus set his daughter down for a moment so he could reach into his pocket for his phone. Fumbling with the screen icons, he dialed the number.

Detective Bradbury picked up, "Hello, Mr. Kane."

"Drop the phone!" a nearby voice shouted.

Cyrus looked up. Stanislav stood a few feet away. In one hand, he had a tight hold of Terra's shirt collar, and in the other, a gun pointed at Cyrus' head.

"I said drop it!" yelled Stanislav. "Now!"

Cyrus let his phone fall to the ground. He kept his eyes fixed on Stanislav's.

"Now kick it over here." Cyrus did as was told. Stanislav yanked Terra's collar. "Toss yours down with his!"

Her hands trembling, Terra pulled her phone from her pants pocket and dropped it as softly as she could next to her grandfather's. Stanislav stepped on the phones with the heel of his shoe, cracking and destroying them. He kicked them off the ledge of the second floor.

"Where's Ivan?" growled Stanislav. "What did you do with him?"

"If you're talking about your pal, don't worry. He's taking a little nap," said Cyrus.

Cyrus slowly moved his body in front of Mary's and raised his hands overhead in a sign of surrender.

"Listen, we have your money," he said calmly. "Just release my granddaughter and let us go, and I'll give you the twenty grand."

"Where's the money?" asked Stanislav.

"You first have to let us go…"

Stanislav stepped closer and brought the barrel of his gun up to Cyrus' head. "I'm not playing games. You either tell me where my money is now or I blow your brains out in front of them."

"Please don't hurt him!" cried Terra.

"Shut up, brat!" yelled Stanislav.

"It's in the truck," said Terra. "Your money's in the truck. All of it."

Stanislav smacked Cyrus hard across the face with the butt of his gun, knocking him to the ground. "Now get up, Mr. Kane," he said.

____

Zeezoo watched helplessly from the windowsill as Stanislav forced the three back into the room and tied them up. When Ivan awakened, he was sent to Cyrus' truck to retrieve the ransom money. He returned a few minutes later with the bag. Shortly afterward, Cyrus, Mary, and Terra were ushered at gunpoint to the SUV.

Outside the vehicle, Ivan asked Stanislav, "Tell me again. Where are we taking them?"

"To the old cannery plant," answered Stanislav. "That place has been abandoned for years. Get in, and I'll pull up the GPS directions. It's not far from here."

The SUV sped off, and Zeezoo took to the air after it. For about a half mile, he trailed them from behind and kept up, but when they turned onto a main highway, he was cut off by a large tractor-trailer and nearly hit. He regrouped and flew higher to avoid another near miss, but by then he had lost sight of the SUV. He searched for several minutes, but it was gone.

Unsure what to do next, Zeezoo flew to a nearby rooftop to catch his breath and think. He looked about to get his bearings, but it was an area of town where he'd never been before. The only thing he recognized was a city bus coming down the street. He watched it stop in front of a bench near an intersection to let off and pick up passengers.

The bus stop reminded Zeezoo of a friend, someone who might be able to help, and gave him an idea. He leapt from his perch and flew straight up in the air, higher and further than he'd ever flown before, until he could see the horizon in all directions. Seizing a passing gust of wind to stay aloft, he twirled and eventually spotted what he was looking for in the far distance. It was the bright red-and-yellow sign outside Tasty Burger.

Except for a few stray clouds, the skies were mostly clear. Zeezoo raced through the air as fast as he could. He stopped twice to recheck where he was, and in less than ten minutes, he came to rest on one of the picnic tables in front of the popular burger joint.

Like most days, Tasty Burger was busy. Customers were going inside to order and coming out with their food and drinks. A long line of cars was wrapped single file around the building, making their way to the drive-through intercom and pick-up window.

Looking around, Zeezoo noticed something was very different than he remembered. The birds milling about weren't fighting over the scraps of food tossed their way. There was a line of birds not far from the door entrance and another gathered near the tables, but unlike before, there was no bullying by the larger birds, no tussles of any kind. Everyone appeared to be taking turns chasing down the tidbits left behind.

From somewhere nearby, he heard a familiar voice call out his name: "Zeezoo!" He turned around. It was Ace.

"Ace!" said Zeezoo. "It's so good to see you."

Zeezoo's high-flying friend flew to the table and landed next to him. "You too!" he said. "I've missed you, buddy. What are you doing here?"

"I need your help," said Zeezoo. "My friend, the man who owns the farm I grew up on, and his family are in danger. They were taken by force to a place called the cannery plant. Can you tell me where that is?"

"I'm not sure," answered Ace. "But there's someone here who might know. Let me get him." He whistled. Moments later, another larger sparrow fluttered into view and landed beside them. Zeezoo immediately took a step back and raised his wings in self-defense when he saw who it was: Thorn.

"Don't come any closer!" yelled Zeezoo.

"Whoa! Whoa! Relax, buddy," said Ace. "Thorn's not going to hurt you. He's a changed bird. Isn't that right, Thorn?"

"He's right," said Thorn. "I'm sorry for what I did to you before, Zeezoo. Please forgive me."

"What's going on?" asked Zeezoo, his wings still up to protect himself. "I'm confused. Why are things so different around here?"

Ace came closer and put his wing around Zeezoo's shoulders. "It's because of you," he answered.

"What do you mean?" asked Zeezoo, lowering his wings.

"There's a wonderful word that explains it best," said Ace. "The word is *inspiration*. I guess you didn't realize it at the time, but you inspired me and others."

"I don't understand," said Zeezoo.

Ace took a few steps back. "That day, Zeezoo, when you stood up to Thorn, no one around here had ever seen someone do that before. After you left, I got to thinking. Why should we always be afraid and fight for scraps when we can choose to live in harmony with everyone and everything? What you did and said, it was like you snuck up on me and planted a tiny seed in my mind. It took root."

"I had no idea," said Zeezoo.

"How could you know?" said Ace. "You were long gone by then. But anyway, I campaigned for change and convinced the smaller and weaker birds to band together as a group and not give in to bullying. Once I had the small ones organized, it was easy to convince the bigger birds to give up their ways, to end the cycle of intimidation and constant threats. And you can see the results yourself. We take turns and help each other. Everyone now behaves in a more civilized way."

"What you did is incredible, and I'd love to hear more about it," said Zeezoo. "But I have to go. I need to find the cannery plant quickly and help my friends."

Ace turned to Thorn. "Do you have any idea where this cannery is?"

Thorn thought for a moment. "My father took me there once when I was young. He told me the farmers used to bring all kinds of freshly picked food there, and they'd seal it in cans to sell to the grocery stores. The place was legendary. Before they closed it, birds came from all over to dine. The cannery is down by the railroad tracks. I remember where it is."

"How many volunteers do you think you can round up in the next half hour to go on a rescue mission?" asked Ace.

"Maybe fifteen to twenty," answered Thorn.

"Then sound the alarm," said Ace. "Bring back as many men as you can find."

Thorn spread his wings and flew off.

"I don't know what to say," said Zeezoo. "But thank you."

"You'd do the same for me," said Ace. "Friends help friends, no matter what."

Within a half hour, Thorn returned with a militia of twenty sparrows. It included two females, Amelia and Bessie. They formed a line near Ace and awaited his instructions.

20

"Why not kill us back at the motel?" asked Cyrus.

A trickle of blood seeped from the corner of his mouth. Both of his blackened eyes were nearly swollen shut. He stood with his hands secured behind his back, slumped over and tied to an iron ventilation pipe along a wall in what once had been a food processing building at the cannery. Since their arrival, Ivan had beaten him unmercifully.

Stanislav finished tying Mary and Terra to a short stack of busted wooden pallets. They were made to sit a few feet apart from each other with their hands tightly bound behind their backs.

"I admit it was tempting," said Stanislav. "But in a sprawling deserted place like this, there's less chance we'll attract witnesses. Plus, if the cops are unable to find bodies, they can't prove a crime was committed. You'll have simply vanished. Even if they arrest me, the case will be easy to defend in court."

The three were held in a massive room with lofty wooden columns and exposed beams. It was filled with scattered debris and large outdated metal objects, pieces of aged industrial equipment once used in the canning process of local fruits and vegetables. Machinery too heavy to move and items that weren't salvageable or worth selling had been left behind to gather dust when the canning operation had closed.

Ivan stood guard with his gun by an open doorway while Cyrus struggled, twisting his hands back and forth in an attempt to free himself.

"You have your money, all of it," Cyrus said wearily. "Please, I'm begging you…please. Let my daughter and granddaughter go. There's no reason to hurt them. You can do whatever you want with me, but let them go."

"Do you really think I'm going to leave any loose ends behind?" asked Stanislav. "Anyway, this is your fault, Mr. Kane. If you had just followed instructions and hadn't tried to be a hero, your loved ones wouldn't be here now."

"That's not true!" yelled Terra. "None of this is my grandpa's fault. It's yours! You helped keep my mom hooked on drugs, and you're the one who kidnapped her. I saw how you tried to cheat her out of money. We're in this old dirty place because of you. Just you!"

"What are you planning to do?" asked Cyrus.

Stanislav took a lighter out of his pants pocket and lit a cigarette. After taking a deep prolonged puff, he blew several smoke rings that drifted softly across the room.

"I've got an idea," he responded. He picked up a grubby rag from the floor and held his lit lighter beneath it. The cloth burst into flames.

Stanislav bowed his head. With eyes closed, he recited a Bible verse. "And the Lord God formed man of the dust of the ground and breathed into his nostrils the breath of life, and man became a living soul." Looking up, he added, "Life is strange, isn't it? All this nonsense and struggle, and in the end, there is but one truth. A man is as written. It's ashes to ashes, dust to dust. The time has come for you to say goodbye."

The flock of sparrows took flight with Thorn leading the way. Ascending above the buildings and trees, they made their way across town, turning left at the railroad tracks and following them several miles, until they spotted an immense smokestack made of brick in the distance.

"There it is," said Thorn.

They came to rest atop a tin-roofed structure adjacent to the smokestack. There were various buildings on the cannery grounds as well as an elevated water tank. The railway siding that led onto the property lay covered in weeds. Here and there, stacks of weathered crates were piled haphazardly.

Ace gave orders to the group. "Spread out, everyone, and search this place from top to bottom. Remember, we're looking for three people—two adults and one kid. There might be predators around, so choose a lookout partner, and go in pairs. Be safe, and whistle if you find anything. Zeezoo, come with me."

The sparrows flew off in all directions.

Not long after, Ace and Zeezoo heard a series of high-pitched whistles coming from the far side of one of the buildings. They rushed to investigate and found Amelia and Bessie perched on an old semi-trailer near what looked like a large distribution facility. There was an open loading bay with a vehicle parked inside.

"This looks like something," said Amelia.

"It's the black SUV they were taken away in," said Zeezoo. He flew inside the loading bay and landed on the hood to get a closer look. "They can't be too far away."

"Good job, ladies!" said Ace.

Amelia and Bessie flew down, landed on the dirty pavement next to the SUV, and surveyed the area.

Pointing her wing, Bessie said, "I see footprints. It looks like more than one person got out of the car. They go off in this direction. Maybe if we follow them, they'll lead us to your friends."

Together, the sparrows took flight and followed the tracks to the rear of another building, where a door had been left ajar. Eager to check it out, they swooped down to enter, but Zeezoo spotted Ivan standing guard just inside the doorway with a gun.

Zeezoo yelled to the others, "Hold up!"

The four sparrows circled back and regrouped on a nearby rooftop. "What's the problem?" asked Ace.

"That guy's one of the kidnappers," said Zeezoo.

"They must be holding your friends somewhere in there," said Ace. "We need to take a quick look inside to make sure."

They flew to a long row of windows high on the side of the building and peered in, but the room was too dark, and the glass panes were covered in a thick brown grimy film. Some of the windows had been boarded up.

"I'm going in," said Zeezoo. "I need one of you to distract Ivan while I slip past him. He saw me earlier at the motel, and we can't risk him becoming suspicious."

"Leave it to me," said Ace.

Ace flew off and disappeared behind the building. A few moments later, he returned with something alive squirming in his beak. It was a good-sized spider with long legs and a hairy body.

"This should do the trick," he mumbled, talking with his mouth stuffed.

Using his speed, Ace dive-bombed the doorway and dropped the spider onto Ivan's head. He raced back to the others in the blink of an eye. The sparrows watched Ivan twitch and brush his bald head nonchalantly. The spider crawled onto Ivan's ear then his face. There was a shriek, not unlike that of a frightened child, and Ivan slapped himself wildly.

Zeezoo saw his chance. Flying low, a foot or so above the ground, he zipped past Ivan's legs. Beyond him lay a cavernous, dimly lit room. He landed on a metal pipe and took a second to let his eyes adjust. A man's voice came from the far end.

"When nightfall comes, I'm going to set this place ablaze. A building this old should burn to the ground in a matter of minutes." Zeezoo recognized the voice; it belonged to Stanislav. "By the time the fire-fighters arrive, there'll be nothing left but embers."

Zeezoo flew closer but stayed out of sight. He saw Cyrus, Terra, and Mary tied up. Stanislav was pacing.

Mary began to cry. "It's my fault. Please forgive me," she said. Tears streamed down her cheeks.

"Calm yourself, woman," said Stanislav. "It won't be a painful death. You'll die breathing in the thick smoke before the flames lap at your skin and cremate you."

Zeezoo had heard enough. He sped as fast as he could out of the building. Ace and the girls were waiting for him on the rooftop.

"We need to do something!" said Zeezoo. "The other kidnapper is going to burn down the building with my friends inside. He has them tied up."

"I'm not sure we can prevent it from happening by ourselves. Our size is a problem," said Ace. "Tell me, Zeezoo, do you know any other people, someone like your friends, who can help free them?"

"There is one person," said Zeezoo. "But I don't think they'd understand me even if I could find them."

"You have to at least try," said Ace. "Don't waste time talking and hurry. Do your best. While you're gone, the rest of us will work on freeing your friends."

Ace turned to Amelia and Bessie. "Go find Thorn and the others. Tell them to meet us back here pronto."

"I'll return as quickly as I can," said Zeezoo.

"Good luck, my friend," said Ace.

Zeezoo fluffed his feathers and took to the air, flying as high as he could. By now it was late afternoon. The world below him was bathed in a warm golden hue.

As he searched the horizon for familiar landmarks, he thought back on the trips into town he had taken with Cyrus. Before he'd met Elin, the old man had been the most important person in his life. He remembered that one rainy morning in the truck when he'd first met Terra. She had come running out of a large building with her grandfather; he could see it in his mind.

There were a few moments of hesitation when the maze of activity, the hum of cars and people flowing in all directions, disoriented him, but with determination and a little bit of luck, Zeezoo found the main road into town. He followed it and not long after came to rest on a lamppost directly across the street from the Children and Family Services' administrative center. Someone leaving the building held the door open for a group of people going in. Zeezoo raced in behind them and looked around.

He landed on a desk cluttered with papers.

Roberta Johnson was talking on the phone. "I have the child's case file…Yes, of course. I'll go over it in more detail when we meet." She looked up and, after a short silence, said, "I need to go. Something has come up…Yes, I'll call you back."

She hung up, paused for a second, and said, "I know you. I've seen you before. You live on the Kane farm. Are you Zeezoo?"

Zeezoo chirped twice then flew to the front door and back again to her desk.

"I'm not sure what's going on, Zeezoo, but if you're here, where is the rest of your family, Cyrus and Terra?"

Zeezoo hopped about frantically, tossing a pencil and some official-looking documents onto the floor. He leapt up onto Roberta's shoulder and tugged hard at her hair, before flying off to the door a second time. He landed atop the exit handle and waited.

Roberta got up, walked to the front door, and looked out. "What are you trying to tell me?" she asked.

The two stared at each other. Nothing more was said.

After several moments passed, the social worker walked back to her desk. She grabbed her purse and cell phone. On the way out the door, she made a call. "Hello, Detective Bradbury. This is Roberta Johnson. I think something has happened."

———

The sun's last light of the day bathed the cannery in an orange-and-red afterglow that soon gave way to darkness.

A hushed stillness fell over the room.

Stanislav had fashioned a torch out of a short wooden stick and dirty rags. He flicked open his lighter and lit the end. In seconds the cloth caught fire, illuminating the room with a menacing radiance.

The flame also cast light on a group of sparrows in the rafters above Stanislav. Terra was the first to notice them. She nudged her mother and motioned with her eyes for her grandfather to look up. Then she felt something behind her tugging at the taut knot of rope binding her wrists. She leaned back and glanced over. Four sparrows were pulling hard on Mary's rope too, trying to loosen it with their beaks. Cyrus nodded to signal "yes"—the sparrows were working to untie him as well.

Without drawing attention to herself, Terra wriggled her hands back and forth. She felt the sparrows move with her as she twisted and pulled.

Next to Stanislav was a small pile of planks and loose debris he had gathered from around the room. He touched the torch to the pile. There was a crackling sound and sparks. The debris flared.

Cyrus raised his head. "Tell me. Do you believe in heaven and hell, Stanislav? Because you know where you're going to spend eternity after this."

With the flames rising higher and spreading in the center of the room, Stanislav walked over to the old man and stood in front of him. He brought his face close.

"It's only real if you believe in hell," said Stanislav. "Believing makes it so. But me, I have my own faith. I believe in the here and now. What else is there?"

"There are those in this world whose hearts are merciful and soar above the rest," said Cyrus. "And then there's low-life idiots and scum like you."

Cyrus looked straight into Stanislav's eyes and spat in his face.

"I've had enough of your mouth!" growled Stanislav. He raised his gun and pointed the barrel inches from Cyrus' forehead. "I think I'll just end your pathetic existence now!"

The gun went off. Mary screamed.

Ivan came running.

Gray billowing smoke filled the room as the fire quickly spread along the floor, the flames growing higher. Shielding his eyes and coughing, Ivan stood a few yards from the blaze, his gun drawn, hesitant to the step further into what would soon be an inferno.

Stanislav lay on his back, his eyes open, but dazed.

Terra had come up behind Stanislav and struck him over the head with a block of wood just as he pulled the trigger. Cyrus was shot through the shoulder. He grimaced in pain as Terra worked to loosen his hands, which were still bound to the iron pipe.

"Get back where you were!" Ivan yelled from the other side of the fire, his gun pointed at Terra.

Able to pry himself free, Cyrus rushed to Mary. Her hands had been untied, but she was too weak to move. He lifted her and looked back. Terra stood over Stanislav, his gun on the floor beside him. She reached down to get it, and Stanislav's eyes came to life. He grabbed her arm. Screaming, Terra fought him. She kicked him in the stomach and broke loose.

"Run, Terra! Run!" yelled Cyrus.

A surging wall of fire had begun to block the way out. Terra found a gap in the flames and leapt through it. She ran past Ivan before he had a chance to react.

"Don't let her get away!" shouted Stanislav.

Ivan gave chase.

Terra ran out into the night air with Ivan right behind. He dove for her, missed, and landed on his face. She sprinted to a nearby warehouse and tugged at a back door to hide inside, but it was padlocked. She ducked around the corner and spotted an access ladder attached to the outside wall that led to the roof.

She quickly moved on, but at the end of the pathway beside the warehouse was a barbed-wire fence and tall stacks of old wooden crates. Terra was boxed in. Hearing Ivan's footsteps, she rushed back to the ladder.

It was dark except for a bit of moonlight. The steel ladder proved to be rickety. Rusted and detached from the wall in places, it shuddered under Terra's weight. She lost her grip and nearly fell. Ivan heard the metal clanking, followed the noise, and spotted Terra halfway up. He climbed after her.

The warehouse rooftop was more than three floors above the ground with no safety railing—nothing between it and the sky. Along the center ridge was a row of rusted turbines used for ventilation as well as a stairwell door that led inside.

Panting, Ivan stepped onto the roof. "I've got you now," he said. "There's no other way back down."

Terra yanked hard on the stairwell door, but it wouldn't budge. She was trapped. Ivan now stood a few feet from her. Panicking, she tried to run around him back to the ladder, but he caught her arm.

"Get off me!" she screamed.

Ivan dragged Terra, punching and kicking, to the edge of the roof. He lifted her over the side. "That's a long way down, isn't it?" he said with a laugh. "I don't think you'll survive the fall."

Terra had a hold of his shirt. "If you let go, I'm taking you with me."

Ivan tried to shake Terra off, but she maintained her grip. She kicked him in the knees; he lost his balance for a moment and stumbled backward. Reaching out, she wrapped her arms firmly around his neck and wouldn't let go.

Terra cried out, "Help me, somebody! He's going to kill me! Help!"

Ivan thrashed and fought to get Terra off. With her locked tightly onto him, he retreated from the roof's edge. They struggled. She dug her nails into his neck and bit down hard on his ear. He howled in pain.

Finally, Ivan was able to force Terra off of him. He slammed her onto the rooftop and pulled out his gun. "That's it," he said. "I should give you a chance to say a few last words, but I don't think I will."

He pointed the gun at Terra. There was movement, a fluttering. From somewhere in the darkness, a flock of sparrows had descended. They were on Ivan en masse, pecking his eyes and clawing his face. He swung at them wildly, spun around, and took several steps back. The last one was a step too far.

Cradling Mary in his arms, Cyrus picked his way through the thick smoke and blinding flames toward the door. Covered in blood, he stumbled forward.

In the middle of the burning room stood Stanislav.

He came at Cyrus hard, knocking him onto his backside and sending Mary sprawling. The two men exchanged violent blows and wrestled, rolling across the floor, in and out of the flames. Despite being hurt, Cyrus fought with everything he had, but Stanislav soon gained the upper hand. He pummeled Cyrus until he was nearly unconscious and thrust his gun in the older man's face.

"Now I'm going to finish what I started," growled Stanislav.

There was a sudden thunderous rumble from above. Stanislav looked up. Engulfed in flames, the columns, beams, and entire roof were about to cave in. He sprang to his feet, but in an instant, it all came crashing down.

Cyrus lay buried.

For a moment, he felt himself floating away, like a tiny speck of ash on a spring wind. He closed his eyes and allowed death to embrace him. It was only then, in the surrender, that he understood for the first time, life and what it meant to live. In the end, the world was little more than bright sparks and burning embers. All he could hope to contribute was his own light.

Cyrus heard familiar voices. There were hands. He felt them tugging at his body and lifting him higher. A final breath merged with time, and what remained was a vast stillness and peace he never knew. He opened his eyes and gasped.

The first thing he saw was the stars. He was lying on his back. Kneeling beside him were Mary and Terra. Tears flowing down their cheeks, they took turns kissing him. Behind them, the fire raged, illuminating black and gray plumes of smoke. The flames spilled from the old cannery building as if from a fountain.

"Welcome back." The voice belonged to Roberta Johnson. Out of breath, she stood next to his daughter and granddaughter. Her face and clothes were blackened with soot. "I thought we'd lost you."

Cyrus sat up groggily. "How did you know where to find us?"

"A friend of yours led me to you," Roberta said. She pointed to a group of sparrows resting on a stack of wooden crates nearby. One leapt up and flew to Cyrus, landing on his good shoulder. It was Zeezoo. The social worker extended her hand and helped Cyrus to his feet.

"Thank you," he said.

Mary threw her arms around her father. "I'm so sorry, Dad. I never meant for any of this," she said, sobbing.

"It's okay, dear," said Cyrus, wincing. "I'm sorry too, for everything. I could have done better. I love you."

"I love you too," said Mary. She held on to her father tightly.

Suddenly, Terra screamed.

Stanislav had emerged from the fire like some hellish creature from the center of the earth. His entire body set ablaze, he staggered toward them, pointing his gun.

A deafening shot rang out.

"That's quite enough," said Roberta. She put her revolver back in a holster inside her blazer and looked at the others. "Why are you staring? I have to work in some pretty rough neighborhoods."

Stanislav lay facedown on the ground.

Crying sirens echoed in the distance.

21

One Month Later

An easterly morning breeze caressed the trees, softly rustling the leaves. The nest was empty. Zeezoo landed on a pine branch near the hole and sighed. It had been several weeks since he had last seen his children.

After the fire at the cannery, Zeezoo and Elin's chicks grew into young fledglings, ready to fly. Two of their boys, Camillo and Dian, were determined to explore the world beyond the woods and make a fresh start for themselves in town. Elin flew off with her sons to help them get settled into their new surroundings. It also gave her a reason to visit her sisters. She was due to return to Zeezoo and the woodland any day.

The two girls, Arriane and Beatrix, couldn't imagine life anywhere else. They loved everything about the woods and never wanted to leave, but they too knew it would be best if they spread their wings and struck out on their own. Promising to return one day, they flew off together to find other forested areas in the county. They were last seen flying above the nearby creek, following its course.

As for Skeeter, well, he never told anyone what his plans were or where he was going. One minute he was perched on the edge of the nest, quietly preening his wings, and the next he was gone.

That afternoon, Terra showed up after school like she always did to check on the young sparrows. She scrambled up the tree, peered inside the hole, and saw the nest was bare. All that remained of the fledglings were a few stray down feathers.

"Aw. I'm very sorry, Zeezoo," said Terra. She had observed the chicks' rapid growth from the beginning and knew the day was coming when they'd leave the nest. "Sparrows grow up so fast. I wish your babies had stayed little forever. I liked seeing them."

Zeezoo gave her a peck on the cheek.

Thereafter, Terra continued to take walks into the woods to visit him and share her thoughts about life, but not as often as she once did.

Now, as Zeezoo stood perched on the pine branch staring at the nest, he thought about Terra and a great many other things. His mind wandered back and forth through time. He remembered little moments, the wind under his wings, a smile on the face of a friend.

Zeezoo's thoughts were interrupted. He heard twigs snap in the dense brush a short distance away. Someone was approaching. He flew to a nearby limb, closer to the ground, to see who it might be. There were several voices, one of which he recognized immediately. It belonged to Angel. The raccoon was speaking in a loud, clear manner like he was some kind of tour guide.

"And now we are approaching the home of..." said Angel. He emerged from behind a clump of thick bushes into the small clearing around the pine. "Oh! There you are, Zeezoo. I was just telling the kids about you."

Huddled behind Angel were three little raccoons. They were quite young and identical in every way. "I don't think you've met my daughters yet," said Angel. "Say hello to Mr. Zeezoo, girls."

"Hellooo, Mr. Zeezoo," said all three girls in unison. They formed a line and sat beside their father.

"Hello, girls," said Zeezoo. "So, Angel, what brings you by today?"

"The wife needed a break from the kids and me," answered Angel. "She kicked us out of the den for a while, so she can rest. I'm taking my girls on a little sightseeing stroll through the woods, so they can burn off some energy and learn where everything is."

The girl on the end raised her paw. "Mr. Zeezoo, can I ask you a question?"

"Sure. What is it?"

"Our daddy says you know the cat skinner. Is it true?" she asked.

One of her sisters chimed in. "Yeah. Are you really friends with him? The cat skinner is scary."

Angel interrupted them. "What did I tell you girls on the way over here? I specifically said not to bother Mr. Zeezoo with questions about the cat skinner."

"Sorry, Dad," said all three in unison.

"It's okay. I understand their curiosity," said Zeezoo. He addressed the girls. "What your dad told you is true. The cat skinner and I are very close." He gave Angel a wink.

"All right," said Angel. "Since you didn't do what I asked, which of you can tell Mr. Zeezoo here what the most important thing is you've learned about the cat skinner?"

All three raised their paws and spoke at the same time. "The cat skinner only comes after bad little boys and girls who don't mind their parents," recited the girls. "He won't eat you if you're good."

Zeezoo tried hard not to laugh. In just a matter of weeks, news of the mysterious cat skinner had spread throughout the woods, and his legend had grown exponentially. The fierce fictional beast had become an enduring part of local lore, and his exploits were used to explain strange bumps in the night and all types of supernatural phenomena. Plus, in addition to cats and other large stealthy predators, the cat skinner was now said to have an insatiable appetite for naughty children.

"Let's move on, girls," said Angel. "We've got more places to see. Say goodbye."

"Goodbye, Mr. Zeezoo," said the three girls. "It was nice to meet you." They quickly lined up behind their father.

"Goodbye," said Zeezoo. "Enjoy the day!" He flew back up to his perch near the nest.

With his daughters in tow, Angel hurried off into the thick underbrush, picking up where he'd left off earlier, telling the girls adventurous stories and pointing out prominent landmarks as they went. Zeezoo listened in, but the raccoon's voice soon receded and disappeared.

Alone again, Zeezoo felt restless.

Further in the distance, Zeezoo heard Cyrus starting up the new tractor. Its distinctive rumble had a way of echoing through the woods like a thunderstorm. Interested in seeing what his friend was up to, he flew to the top of a tall oak alongside the field, arriving in time to watch a flock of red-winged blackbirds take to the sky. He followed the arc of their flight into the blue, and then something else caught his eye. A tiny speck darted in and out of the white clouds.

Zeezoo watched it tumble and soar high in the air above him. The freewheeling movements were playful, young, and aggressive. It was a small bird, possibly another sparrow, but too far away for him to make out what it might be. When the unidentified bird eventually zipped behind a cloud and didn't return, Zeezoo leapt from his perch and flew after it. He needed to get a better look at the bird to make sure it wasn't a threat to his nesting area.

On the other side of the cloud, Zeezoo caught a quick glimpse of the bird, but it dove into the drifting mist and eluded him. He gave chase, but when he emerged from the cloud, all trace of the intruder was gone. He paused for a second and scanned the earth below. The world looked so incredibly peaceful, like a beautiful patchwork quilt. The farm, woods, highway, creek—everything was its own separate bit of decorated cloth, sewn together and forever intertwined with the surrounding countryside, all the way to the horizon and beyond.

Suddenly, Zeezoo felt a tap on his shoulder. "Why are you tailing me?" asked a voice behind him. He spun around and came face-to-face with the mystery bird. It was his son, Skeeter.

"Dad!" said Skeeter.

"Skeeter!" said Zeezoo.

The two embraced, hovering together in the sky.

"Where have you been, Son?" asked Zeezoo.

"I've been flying all over looking for a place I can call home," answered Skeeter. "I've traveled dozens of miles in every direction."

"Were you able to find anything?"

"Yes. I think I've found a great spot. Would you like to see it?"

"Of course," answered Zeezoo.

"Follow me," said Skeeter. He swooped down and winged across the field with his father behind him. They zoomed past Cyrus in his shiny new air-conditioned tractor and, soon after, came to rest atop the chicken coop. The hens, Eeny, Meeny, and Miny, were busy eating mealworms.

"Is this it?" asked Zeezoo.

"No," said Skeeter. "But we're close." He flew to the rim of the chickens' water bowl and took a long sip. "It's up there." He pointed to the barn as he quenched his thirst. "Come on. Let me show you," he said. The fledgling flew to an opening in the wood, the same hole high on the barn that was in need of mending. Inside were the remnants of an old abandoned nest.

Zeezoo landed next to his son. Together, side by side, they stood at the edge of the hole and looked around. In a patch of sunlight on the ground below, Edgar lay half asleep. He glanced up, and his tail began to flick.

"That cat over there is crazy," said Skeeter. "So what do you think about this place, Dad?"

"It's perfect," said Zeezoo.

Cyrus brought the tractor to a stop in the middle of the field, stepped out of the cab, and knelt to get a better look at the corn seedlings. He inspected several seedlings closely for signs of pest damage and disease. The individual leaves were dark green and healthy. He smiled and stood up; it appeared the corn crop was off to a good start. He needed to add some nutrients to the soil, but with the right amount of rainfall and a bit of luck going forward, the harvest was on track to be exceptional.

His phone buzzed. Cyrus retrieved it from his jeans pocket and took a look. It was a text message from Terra. She had attached a selfie of herself with her three friends, Nikki, Desiree, and Cleo. All four girls were mugging for the camera next to Lizzie in front of the mare's stall. He laughed. The girls were spending the entire day on the farm with Terra and having a sleepover later that night.

He texted back, "Great pic!"

Cyrus climbed into the tractor and drove back to the farmhouse. He parked it near the barn. A man in white overhauls was waiting for him by the front steps.

"Hey, there, Mr. Kane," said the man. "I finished lettering and painting the sign. Do you want to look it over and tell me what you think before I leave?"

"Sure, Mitch," answered Cyrus. "I'm sure you did a good job, but let's go see." Mitch Inglehart was a professional sign painter, one of the best in the area. Cyrus had hired him to create a fancy new sign for the farm out by the main road.

As they neared the highway, Mitch said, "I think what you're planning to do here is a great thing."

"Thank you," said Cyrus. "If I've learned anything, it's that life is short and tomorrow isn't guaranteed. Before my time is up on this earth and they bury me, I want to leave behind a little light, something that has a chance to live on long after I'm gone."

The two men stood in front of the new sign. In large cursive letters it read, GRACIE'S FARM. Beneath it said, EVERYONE IS WELCOME! Around the words, Mitch had painted colorful flowers and framed it all within exquisite scrollwork.

"It's absolutely wonderful!" said Cyrus. "You've exceeded my expectations."

Mitch reached down and picked up something off the ground near the sign. He handed it to Cyrus. "I don't know what you want to do with this," said Mitch. It was the old ratty KEEP OUT sign.

Cyrus laughed. "It's trash." He tossed it back to the ground. "Do me a favor. Take it with you when you go, and throw the thing out."

Just then, a familiar car turned onto the dirt road and came to a stop next to them. The window rolled down. It was Roberta Johnson.

"Good day, gentlemen," she said. "Mr. Kane, I have the young lady with me I was telling you about earlier."

Cyrus could see there was a child roughly Terra's age riding in the backseat. "Fantastic!" he said. "We were expecting you. I'll meet up with you both in a minute."

He finished discussing a few minor details regarding a future sign-painting project with Mitch, shook his hand, and walked back to the house. Roberta was waiting for Cyrus next to her car; its trunk was open. Beside the social worker stood a young girl, clutching a small brown-and-white teddy bear.

"Hello again," said Roberta. "I'd like you to meet Brooke."

Cyrus extended his hand. "It's a pleasure to meet you, Brooke. We're excited to have you come live with us. I think you'll enjoy it here. If you need anything—anything at all—don't hesitate to tell me."

"Yes, sir, Mr. Kane," Brooke said shyly. She saw his hand but didn't take it.

Cyrus could see the distrust in the girl's eyes. Brooke had a tight grip on her bear. "Please, you can call me Grandpa," he said. "Or if you want, just yell, 'Hey, old man!' and I'll come running." He chuckled. In the trunk of Roberta's car were two suitcases. He took them out and set them on the ground near the front steps.

Terra and her three friends came running out of the barn. Laughing, they made a beeline for Brooke and gathered closely around her. Roberta introduced the seven-year-old to everyone. When she was done, the girls converged on Brooke and gave her a group hug.

"Come on, Brooke! Let me show you your room. It's next to mine," said Terra, grinning. "We're going to have lots of fun!" She grabbed Brooke's hand, and all five girls went running toward the farmhouse.

"Wait!" said Cyrus. "I want to take a few pictures of everybody first."

"Oh, yeah!" said Terra. "We have a brand-new computer and printer. Grandpa bought some photo paper, and he wants to put pictures of us up on the wall."

The girls posed together near the front steps. Cyrus snapped several pictures of them with his phone. "Say cheese!" he said. Brooke was smiling. When he finished, the girls turned and darted into the house.

Cyrus then noticed something he hadn't seen before. Roberta had a big smile on her face. The normally reserved social worker couldn't hide the fact she was pleased. He studied her expression. She was beautiful.

He thought for a moment and said, "Roberta, I don't think I've ever shown you around the farm. Would you like to see more? I could give you the nickel tour."

"I'd like that very much," said Roberta. "First, though, I want to thank you for agreeing to open your home to Brooke. I'm delighted you chose to become a foster parent."

She paused, glanced around, and added, "And I must say, the entire farm is different. You've changed quite a few things since the first time I was here. Everything looks incredibly clean and organized."

"There's new paint on the barn and farmhouse, and every building has a new roof. Things I've long neglected have been repaired and upgraded," said Cyrus. "It's a work in progress, and we're just getting started. There's a lot left to do. Come. Let me show you."

Cyrus led Roberta past Grace's old vegetable garden, now tilled and green with the corn seedlings that refused to die. In the end, a fourth of the seeds that Terra planted had germinated. Gaps in the soil were painstakingly filled with newer seeds, and planted alongside the corn was a row of daisies, one of his wife's favorite flowers; they were just beginning to bloom.

Beyond the garden was an open parcel of land. Cyrus stopped. "We're going to expand the farm's capacity using the latest advances in agricultural technology, plant more acres, and bring in livestock," said Cyrus. "And right here…this is where the money we earn, all the profits, will go. On this spot where we're standing, I intend to build a state-of-the-art shelter for mothers and their children who are victims of domestic abuse."

Roberta stared at the plot of land, silent. She appeared stunned. After a moment or two, she reached for Cyrus' hand and held it. "I don't know what to say," she said. "What an incredible idea and gift! What an amazing man you are."

Cyrus and Roberta heard a door slam, followed by a lot of giggling. Soon there was a stampede of young feet running toward them. "There they are," cried Terra.

Out of breath, the pack of girls congregated around the two adults. Terra acted as their spokesperson. "Ms. Johnson, we were wondering…Grandpa says he's going to let us make s'mores around a campfire after supper. Can you stay and eat s'mores with us tonight?"

"Girls," said Cyrus, "I'm sure Ms. Johnson has more important things to do—"

"I love s'mores," Roberta interrupted him. "But first I have to go home and change my clothes. I'd hate to get sticky marshmallow and melted chocolate all over my nice work suit." She gave the girls a smile.

"Yay!" shouted the girls.

"Let's go play with Thor and Loki," said Terra. The girls turned and ran off. A minute later, they were laughing and giggling in the goat pen.

"Will you walk with me to my car?" asked Roberta. "I've got some follow-up paperwork I need to file at the office."

Cyrus led Roberta back. On the way, they discussed a few details regarding the new shelter. She promised to help him process whatever applications were required for state approval and a license.

Roberta got into her car and rolled down the window. "Have you spoken to Mary about your plans for the shelter?" she asked.

"Yes. She's anxious to return to the farm and help manage things," answered Cyrus. "But first she has to finish serving time for violating her parole. The judge sentenced her to another two years in prison, but we've been told she might get out earlier for good behavior in nine months. Terra and I visit her when we can."

Cyrus leaned over and gave Roberta's forehead a little kiss. "I'm so sorry," he said, hesitantly. "I don't know what came over me."

"I do," said Roberta. She pulled his face closer and kissed him on the cheek. "I'll see you after work. Tell the girls the s'mores are off limits until I get back."

Roberta rolled up the window and started the car. A minute later, she was gone. Brooke's suitcases were still by the front steps. Cyrus took them inside to her room, which smelled of fresh paint. Brooke's teddy bear was propped up in the middle of her bed.

Cyrus went downstairs into the kitchen and poured some coffee. He took a few sips, dumped the rest in the sink, and headed back outside to finish up in the cornfield. On his way to the tractor, he spotted Brooke near the garden. She was by herself, sniffling. He rushed over to find out what had happened.

"What's wrong, Brooke?" asked Cyrus. "Why aren't you with the other girls?"

"Terra is making up fibs," said Brooke. "She says she wants to be my best friend, but friends aren't supposed to lie to each other. My whole life, I've been tricked by people I know, and lied to. I don't like liars."

Cyrus opened his arms, and Brooke let him give her a hug. He felt her body relax. The crying stopped. "What exactly did Terra say that was a lie?" he asked.

"She says there's a bird who lives here who's her friend…a wild bird, not a pet," said Brooke. "She said the bird understands what she's saying, and she talks to it. I kind of believed her at first, but then Terra said the bird and its bird friends saved her life and yours too. I don't believe her. Why would Terra make up a lie like that?"

"Well, sweetheart, everything Terra told you is true," said Cyrus. "We do have a little sparrow on the farm that I rescued and raised from a baby; he's a part of the family. He understands us. I have no idea how he knows what we're saying to him, but he does."

"Really?" said Brooke. "So she's not lying?"

"No," Cyrus replied. "Would you like to meet him and maybe hold him too?"

"Yes."

Cyrus whistled for Zeezoo.

RUSSELL SEBRING is a novelist and poet who grew up in the south. He graduated with a photography degree from the Art Institute of Fort Lauderdale before going on to work as a journalist, independent copywriter, professional photographer, and web designer.

Russell lives within a few miles of Hogwarts Castle at Universal's Islands of Adventure and Cinderella Castle at Walt Disney World in Florida.